Published in 2010 by Marplesi

ISBN 978-0-9566983-3-9

The Reluctant Detective

by

Sinclair Macleod

MARPLESI

Dedication

For Kim and Kirsten with all my love

and in memory of Calum, my wonderful son.

*

Acknowledgements

Thanks go to Kevin Cuthbert and George Mitchell, two former members of Strathclyde Police, who helped me with the details of police procedure. Any mistakes will be mine and nothing to do with those fine gentlemen. Thanks also to Andrew Melvin, his knowledge of the English language and all its nuances was invaluable to me and I hope to you, good reader. The credit for the quiz team name lies squarely with my father-in-law, Paul Slater. My gratitude extends to Audrey Cuthel, who gave me the idea for Alex to have a sex change from the first draft.

Finally, a big thank you to the readers of the first and second drafts, your comments and advice were an enormous help to me in turning this story from jumbled ideas in my head into a readable novel.

*

Disclaimer

The council procedures mentioned in the book are purely for the purposes of the story and don't necessarily reflect the procedures in real life. No slight is intended on the good people of the city council or the work that they do.

Chapter One

"I want you to find who killed my son."

The hot coffee slipped from my hand in slow motion as I watched helplessly, it landed on my desk, splashing the brown liquid everywhere and scalding my chest. I jumped to my feet slightly ahead of Mrs. Kilpatrick, the lady whose words had caused me to make a fool of myself.

*

There are moments in your life, decisions made, actions taken, people you meet or even random chance, that change your life forever. When Mrs. Kilpatrick walked into my office, she brought with her one of those moments.

It had been a day like any other until Mrs. Kilpatrick called. I finished reviewing the paperwork for my latest case. The subject's name was Bill English and he was claiming an insurance payment as the result of an accident at work. He stated that the fall had left him unable to walk properly, that he was unable to work and his daily life had been affected adversely by the injury. His company's insurers had contacted me and asked me to have a look. I followed him over the course of a week and watched as he struggled with a cane into the surgery of his doctor, laboured his way to the Department of Work and Pensions to claim his disability allowance, then score a stunning hat-trick in his weekly five-a-side match. I had photographed his whole performance to accompany my report and his stupidity would cost him his compensation and probably his job.

When I was happy with the paperwork and had printed off the appropriate photographs, I put the whole lot into an envelope, addressed it and put enough stamps on it to get to the General Insurance Company HQ in Peterborough.

It was like a lot of my work since leaving one of the big insurance companies to strike out on my own. For the past two years I had seen every scam in the book and some that weren't in the book; in doing so I helped to save the shareholders a fortune. There had even been a couple of occasions that I proved the claimant to be correct and in truth, they were much more satisfying. My mate Li was always badgering me about being a tool of the "man" but I had to eat, even if I wasn't too proud of myself on occasion.

I was in the middle of closing up for the night; locking drawers, tidying my desk and shutting down my computer when Margaret the office cleaner popped her head round my door.

"Hi, Margaret. I'll be a few more minutes."

"Nae problem, son. How are ye doin'?"

"I'm not too bad, Margaret. How about yourself?"

"Gettin' by, as usual. Have ye got yirsel' a girlfriend or even a boyfriend yet?"

I smiled. I don't know if it is unique to Glasgow but to be single at 29 still seems to be the equivalent of having two heads or six arms; it is regarded as being a totally unnatural state. Margaret was constantly worried about my love life, to a much greater degree than I was myself. Despite my reassurances, she asked about it every time I met her.

"I'm fine, Margaret. I've just been too busy."

"Och, how can ye be too busy to get yirsel a bit o' lovin'?" She added a raunchy emphasis to the last word, laughed and then shook her head at my hopeless situation.

Margaret was seventy years old and loved her job. She was sprightly and enjoyed the social interactions that her fifteen hours a week allowed her. I was about to answer her again when the phone chirped an electronic interruption.

"Hello, Campbell Investigations. How can I help you?" I hoped my irritation at a late call didn't show too much in my voice.

"I would like to speak to Mr. Campbell, please." A refined female voice, she sounded nervous.

"I'm Craig Campbell."

"Is there any chance I can come and see you?"

"How about an appointment tomorrow morning?" I replied, wishing she would agree.

"I was hoping to come right now." Her voice had taken on a slight tone of desperation. "I've been trying to pluck up the courage to do this for a while."

Intrigued, I replied, "OK, can you tell me what it's about?"

"I can't really say over the phone, it's complicated and I'd rather tell you face to face."

"Do you know where my office is?"

"It's in Bridgeton isn't it?"

"That's right. It's the Templeton Business Centre, off Glasgow Green."

"Is that in the old carpet factory?"

"That's right. I'm on the second floor."

"I'll be there in about fifteen minutes. My name is Anne Kilpatrick."

"That's fine. I'll see you then." The phone line went dead. This was an unusual start to a business relationship; my clients were normally insurance companies or businesses needing help with insurance issues. I rarely received individual clients.

The Templeton Carpet Factory was built in 1889 and is modelled on the Doge's Palace in Venice. The facade is made of pale red brick with unusual detail crafted in yellow and blue. It is a stunning example of Victorian architectural eccentricity and is one of Glasgow's most recognisable buildings. Converted to a combination of small offices and apartments in 1984, it sits on the edge of Glasgow Green, an open park in the heart of the city on the north bank of the River Clyde.

The park itself is a significant part of the history of the city, a place where animals grazed, criminals were executed, and washing was hung to dry, where the Glasgow Fair brought joy to the citizens and where the struggle for social justice was voiced. Today it is a place for children to play, a venue for sporting and music events, the home of the museum of the people of Glasgow and a haven in the city where the community can relax.

My office was one of the smallest units in the building but it suited my limited needs. I had filled it with a collection of second-hand furniture. A solid if unspectacular desk, a decent office chair for myself and two comfortable visitors' chairs covered in an unattractive shade of green. There was also an ugly brown and cream filing cabinet that was straight from the BBC series "Life on Mars", an ugly relic of a tasteless era. I had abandoned trying to keep plants as my ability to turn a healthy green beauty into an ugly brown stick had already killed off three Aglaonemea. The only decoration was a photograph of my Ducati ST4s, sad I know.

I filled up my two-cup kettle, from a bottle of water I kept on a tray next to it, put it on to boil and waited for Anne Kilpatrick to arrive. I pondered on what she might need from me. I had occasional enquiries from people who were looking for missing pets, or were convinced that their neighbours were aliens. I had avoided the vast majority of them and definitely dodged the requests to spy on cheating spouses; they were too much hassle and could get messy. I hoped that my visitor didn't need a service of that kind.

She arrived within the fifteen minutes. She was in her early sixties, slim and petite with greying brown hair. Her features were still striking, with high prominent cheek bones and an elegant line to her chin. I could see the stunning beauty of her younger years had aged gracefully into a distinguished and dignified lady. Although there were lines around her eyes and mouth, her skin looked clear and healthy. She wore a long grey coat with a slightly military cut, a crimson red scarf and matching leather gloves. She held herself well but there was an innate sadness about her and an impression of nervous anticipation in the way she moved.

I offered my hand, "Mrs. Kilpatrick. Hi, come in. Can I get you a tea or coffee?"

"Tea, please. Thank you for seeing me at such short notice."

"Have a seat. Milk and sugar?"

"Just milk, please."

She made herself comfortable while I poured the tea and coffee. I handed her the tea and I sat down.

"Now, how can I help you?"

*

She rushed to help me as I held the scalding shirt away from my chest. "Oh I'm so sorry, I didn't mean to shock you." She fussed over me in a motherly fashion.

"That's OK, it was my own stupid fault. I'll go and change. I'll just be a couple of minutes."

I grabbed my sports bag from beside the desk. I always carried a change of clothes as I was never comfortable on my motorbike in a shirt and tie.

I rushed to the toilet and soaked some paper towels in cold water. After taking off my shirt, tie and trousers, I placed the towels on my chest to take some of the heat out of the painful red area. When the pain had subsided a little,

I dressed in my faded jeans and 'Ramones' T-shirt. Not standard business apparel but for the moment there was no other option. I walked back to my office wondering if my client would still be there.

My clumsy stupidity hadn't scared her away and she sat patiently waiting for my return. I sat in the other visitor's chair as my own was damp from the remnants of the coffee. Mrs. Kilpatrick had obviously cleaned the desk for me. I picked up a note pad and pen in an effort to look a little more professional.

"Are you all right?" she asked.

"I'm fine, I'll need to dry clean the suit but I'll survive." I changed tack. "Mrs. Kilpatrick, I'm not sure how I can help you. I'm not really that kind of investigator. The work I do is all for insurance firms and I've never investigated a death or anything remotely like it before."

"Mr Campbell, I am desperate. I don't know what else to do. I was drawn to your advert in the Yellow Pages and I thought maybe it was a sign. I've been trying to get some resolution for nearly a year and I need someone to help me." Her voice began to crack and she wrung her hands in an agitated emphasis of her words.

"Have you spoken to the police?"

"I have tried to convince them that there was something wrong but they say there is nothing to indicate anything other than an accidental death."

"Perhaps it would be better if you start at the beginning."

She tried visibly to compose herself. "My son Rory was killed by a train near Hyndland Station on 20th December last year. It was the first train of the day and the driver didn't even see him. The post-mortem found that there was alcohol in his blood; they thought he was drunk and had fallen or even lain down on the track."

"Why would you suspect foul play? It sounds like a Christmas night out gone tragically wrong."

She reacted angrily. "Because, Mr. Campbell, my son didn't touch alcohol, ever. This is what the police can't seem to understand. He hated it because of what it did to his dad and to our family." Her face had reddened slightly.

I was surprised at the force of conviction that her words held. "What happened to his father?"

"My husband was a doctor, a local GP. He worked long hours, he was extremely stressed by the pressures of his practice and the administration involved in keeping it going. He began to drink a glass of wine every night, then it became a bottle and within a year it was a bottle of spirits. I pleaded with him to stop but it had a grip of him and he told me I didn't understand, that it was his only relief. As a result of his drinking he misdiagnosed a patient, who then passed away. He was facing a hearing in front of the General Medical Council and the possibility of a criminal investigation. He would have been struck off but he never got to the hearing. He took an overdose of diazepam and codeine, washed down with a bottle of whisky. He fell into a coma for two days. Rory and I were at his bedside when he died." The strain of reciting the story was reflected on her face.

"What age was Rory when this happened?"

"He was fifteen, thirteen years ago now."

"How did you and Rory cope after his father's death?"

"I went back to work, I hadn't worked since Rory was born. I think he felt he had lost two parents for a short time, he became withdrawn for a couple of years. It was then that he became interested in art and I think that was therapeutic for him. He gradually got better and by the time he went to university, he was a well-adjusted lad again. The only thing he held on to was that he vowed never to touch alcohol, he was very passionate about it." Tears appeared in her eyes and she reached for her handbag. She lifted a pack of tissues and dabbed away the liquid emotion. "I'm sorry. Rory's death added to what happened to his father have taken their toll. Trying to get justice for Rory is almost all that keeps me going. It's all been too much."

"That's OK, I understand. Is there any other reason you suspect the Rory's death wasn't an accident? Had he mentioned being scared or worried about something?"

"Not really. I hadn't seen him for a couple weeks before his death, just spoken to him on the phone. Isabel, his girlfriend, might know something."

I took a note of her name.

"Where did Rory work?"

"He worked for the council, dealing with PPP tenders for council work." Public Private Partnerships were a government programme to allow private sector companies to build public buildings like schools and hospitals. The contractors build a project and rent it back to the public sector. It is the only idea that the government has to combat years of neglect.

"Mrs Kilpatrick, I'll have a think about it. I don't want to make promises that I can't keep."

"Please Mr. Campbell, I have money if that's what's worrying you." She reached into her handbag and came up with a purse. She opened it and proffered a bundle of cash in my direction. "There's £500 and I can get more if you need it."

"It's not the money, honestly. I don't think I have the resources to help you, I'm a one-man operation."

"Please, take this. If you could even find enough to persuade the police to have another look, that would be a big help. It is so difficult to have this hanging over me. It's like Rory's name is being stigmatised in the same way his father's was. Just another drunk."

I didn't think there was anything I could do but decided that I would take the money from her and return it to her later if I chose to turn her down.

"I'll take the money but please don't get your hopes up that I'll find anything the police couldn't."

She nodded and passed the cash to me. "Thank you Mr. Campbell, it's all I can ask and I am running out of options."

I took down her details and Isabel's number.

She also suggested some work colleagues of Rory's who might be willing to help out. She thanked me again and walked out the office.

I sat for a short time wondering what to do. The poor lady was obviously desperate if she was pinning her hopes on an insurance investigator.

I picked up the phone and dialled the mobile number of my mate Li.

"Hi pal, you need a lift?"

"Certainly do."

"I'll be there in fifteen."

I put on my leathers and closed up the office. The Ducati was calling.

*

Li worked in his family barber shop in Garnethill. He lived just two minutes walk from me and I frequently picked him up on the way home to Partick.

When I walked in he was finishing the artistic styling of a young guy's hair to a look that no woman could resist. At least that's what the customer was hoping.

"Hi Craig. I'll be with you in a couple of minutes."

I sat in a chair and watched him work. He had trained as a hairdresser after working in his father's shop since he was 14. Away from the shop, Li was a ball of mischievous fun but at the salon he applied himself in a professional manner. He was a skilled hairdresser and had begun to change his Dad's traditional barber shop into a high quality hairdresser for men. Mr. Chen had mainly catered for the Chinese community of Glasgow but Li was establishing himself with a cosmopolitan mix of the young and trendy set. His prices were rising as a result and the shop was going from strength to strength.

I'm not sure that Mr. Chen approved but he was in semi-retirement and restricted himself to cutting the hair of his older, more established customers. He had handed over the reins to Li and was gracious enough not to complain.

I met Li after I had an accident with my first motor

bike. A driver kindly pulled out in front of me and allowed me to jump over his bonnet without my bike. I was lucky to have received only a broken leg and damaged tendons in my shoulder. The tendons had refused to heal properly and were too stiff for me to do physiotherapy exercises. A colleague in the insurance company recommended Li to me, as among his other talents, he is a fine acupuncturist. His grandmother had educated Li about the ancient Chinese art and Li had been a willing and enthusiastic learner. He was already very knowledgeable and skilled long before he earned the official qualifications. Our time together during treatments was spent discovering similar tastes and interests. We became firm friends.

The follicular creation complete, the young man paid and headed out into the biting cold of a frosty December day.

"What's new?" Li asked as he began brushing up the strands of cut hair from the shop floor. He normally had a junior trainee in the shop with him but today he was alone as the young man was at college.

"I have had a weird day. A woman came in today and asked me to find who murdered her son."

"You're kidding." Li's broad Glaswegian accent betrayed the fact that he was the third generation of Chen to have lived in Scotland.

"I wish I was."

"What did you say?"

"I've told her I'll think about it."

Li stood poised over the brush and listened avidly as I then proceeded to detail Rory Kilpatrick's story and his mother's concerns.

"Do you think there's anything in it? Do you think that someone could have murdered him?" I could tell that he was fascinated by the possibility of me chasing a murderer.

"I really don't know. She's so convinced that he would never have taken any alcohol and that's what she's basing her suspicions on. He doesn't seem to have any obvious enemies."

"What about the girlfriend? Maybe an insurance job?"

"Maybe, I'll do a little digging on that angle. I'm not sure this is right for me."

Li smiled in his usual playful way when he was about to have a dig at me. "What, worried about working for the good guys for a change? Worried the devil might make a claim on that soul he's bought and paid for?"

"Sorry Li, I can't laugh at this one. I seem to be all the poor woman has and in truth, I'm not much."

"Sorry, mate; foot-in-mouth disease." Li resumed his sweeping and said, "I think you should have a look. You said yourself you might at least be able to check insurance-related stuff and maybe Alex will be able to help you with what the police have discovered up to now."

I had completely forgotten about Alex. Alexandra Menzies had been at university with me and for a short time we were an item. Her degree in Economics had somehow mutated into a job as a Detective Sergeant in Strathclyde Police. We had parted on good terms but I hadn't spoken to her in quite a long time.

"You're right, it's about time Alex made herself useful." I decided to do what I could for Mrs. Kilpatrick, even if it was only to prove to her that the police were correct and that there were no suspicious circumstances.

Li finished tidying up and closed the shop. We headed west, and as I weaved the bike through the traffic on Great Western Road, my mind split between my task and my reflections on my day. We turned into Byres Road and I dropped Li off before heading home.

*

After cooking myself a quick pasta dish, I resolved to make a few calls and get prepared to earn Mrs. Kilpatrick's money.

The first person I decided to call was Alex. We had been together for about a year and despite my feelings, it was never serious on her part. We had drifted apart with no real drama and had remained distant friends. I hadn't spoken to her in a while, although we exchanged Christmas cards and sent a text to each other on our respective birthdays. I wondered how she would react to hearing from me again.

"Alex? Hi, it's Craig."

"Craig, How are you? I haven't spoken to you for ages." She sounded pleased to hear my voice.

"I know, Alex, sorry about that. Am I disturbing you?"

"Only if you call saving me from yet more Christmas shopping disturbing me. I sometimes think I work harder on my days off than I do when I'm at work. Andrew's worse than a woman for wanting to shop. Ow, that's him nipping me."

I hadn't realised that she was with someone. A small regretful thought arrived and departed. "Alex, I'm looking for a favour. Do you remember a case from about a year ago; a young guy was killed on the railway near Hyndland Station?"

"Vaguely. Why, have you got insurance stuff to look into?" she asked in her professional voice.

"Well, kind of. His mother thinks he was murdered and has hired me to investigate for her."

She was now fully focused on what I was saying. "Oh. That could get complicated."

"I know. I was wondering if you could cast your eye over the investigation records and see if there's anything that might have been missed."

"Look Craig, I'm not sure about this. The case is closed and there might be questions if I start poking my nose in, it's not even within our remit. Anything on the railway is the British Transport Police's responsibility."

"I understand all of that. I'm not asking you to give me details, I just want to be sure that every angle was covered and nothing was overlooked. There must be a computer system or something you could check. Even if I can go back to Mrs Kilpatrick and tell her that I'm sure her son's death was accidental; it might give her some peace."

"OK Craig. I might be able to find something for you. I'll see what I can do. I'll give you a ring when I find anything."

"Cheers Alex. Thanks." The conversation had been surprisingly straightforward, old friends catching up. I put the phone down and went to the kitchen and poured myself a glass of Chianti. I took the wine, some cheese and crackers through to the living room and settled down with the phone again. This time I dialled the number Mrs Kilpatrick had given me for Isabel MacLean, Rory's girl friend.

"Hello." A soft Western Isles accent lilted down the line.

"Hi, is that Isabel?"

"Yes, who's speaking?" she was guarded.

"Isabel, my name is Craig Campbell. Mrs Kilpatrick, Rory's mum, gave me your number."

"What for?"

"She's asked me to investigate Rory's death. She doesn't think it was an accident."

"I see." Her tone was cold.

"I was wondering if I could meet you for a chat sometime."

"I suppose so, when?"

"Would tomorrow be convenient?"

"I work in town, could you meet me at lunch time?" Her suggestion was unenthusiastic.

"That would be great. Where?"

"Do you know the Costa Coffee in Royal Exchange Square?"

"Yes, I know the one you mean, on the corner with Queen Street?"

"Close to the corner, yes. Meet me there at 12:15."

"I'll be easy to spot, I'll be wearing motorbike leathers."

"Fine." The phone clicked as she hung up.

Charming, I thought.

I spent the next couple of hours writing out a list of possible questions and contacts while the Kings of Leon played from my Mac. I tried to consider what would help me to discover a bit more about Rory. Was he really the picture of sobriety his mother believed him to be? I could understand him being put off drinking alcohol by his father's addiction and then possibly succumbing due to his own stress. There was also the possibility that he disguised his drinking from his mum in a bid to protect her; maybe on that fateful night he lost control and ended up in the wrong place at the wrong time.

The intrigue and doubt about the case occupied my mind as I lay staring at the bedroom ceiling. I wondered if there really had been a crime committed; who would have harmed him and why? If he was killed, it was by someone very cold and calculating. It didn't feel like a crime of passion; it was a crime of greed or the crime of a psychopath. These thoughts prevented me from getting to sleep until well after 2:00 a.m.

Chapter Two

The next morning at 7:30, my alarm stirred me to consciousness after a restless night. I rose bleary-eyed and went for a cool shower to wash away the confusing thoughts of the early hours. I cut myself with my razor as I shaved, my mind not entirely on the job. I looked at my 29 year-old face. It's on the handsome side of plain, green eyes and dark brown hair, the kind of everyman face that made surveillance easier. I dressed in my Led Zeppelin tee shirt, a pair of Levis and black Converse All Stars for comfort. I wouldn't need a suit today.

Breakfast was a slice of toast and marmalade with a strong, rich Costa Rican coffee to help kick start my mind. My caffeine addiction is my only real vice, apart from the Ducati of course. The beans worked their magic and I began to feel ready to face my first day as a real private eye. I wished I had a movie detective's cool but I was more than a bit nervous about the responsibility I was taking on.

After putting on my leathers, I picked up my helmet,

locked up the flat and headed downstairs. Mrs. Capaldi opened her door as I passed.

"Hey Craig, how are you today?" Despite nearly 50 years in Scotland, Mrs. Capaldi's accent was as strongly Tuscan as the day she arrived even though she had picked up a few Scots phrases along the way.

"Hi, Mrs. Capaldi. I'm good. Kome sta?" It was the only bit of Italian I could remember and Mrs. Capaldi would laugh at my terrible accent every time I said it.

She had arrived in Glasgow in the aftermath of the war, escaping a village that was devastated by the Allied advance. She spoke no English when she arrived and went to live with her uncle who had been in Scotland since before the war. She worked as a seamstress and met her husband, Angelo, at a family wedding. They fell in love immediately and were married in 1950, four years after her arrival. Her son, Lou, was born two years later, followed by his sister, Maria, three years after that. Angelo had passed away many years before I moved into the flat. Her family were frequent visitors; she doted on her seven grandchildren and three great grandchildren.

She had a subtle way of extracting information from people and enjoyed a bit of gentle gossip every now and again. I liked her sense of humour and the sometimes flirtatious twinkle in her eye whenever we chatted. Despite her 75 years, she was a lively and vivacious woman who enjoyed her life to the full.

"Va bene, Craig, va bene. Off to work?" she asked.

"Aye, no rest for the wicked."

"If that's the case you should never leave the office," she laughed.

"I'm not the only one then," I replied. She laughed louder and waved me on my way.

Parking in the West End of Glasgow is a nightmare and the Ducati made perfect sense for me. I can park it close to the door of my tenement and it takes up very little space. I made this my main defence whenever my mother started moaning about me riding a motorcycle and she would always reply with a long sigh. It didn't have to be a 1000cc Italian firebrand but hey, I'm never going to own a Ferrari. I climbed on, turned the key and set off for the office.

*

I arrived at 8.45 and immediately put the kettle on before booting up my computer. I had barely sat down with my second coffee of the day when the office door swung open and a short, red-faced man walked in.

"You Campbell?"

"Excuse me?"

"Are you deaf? I asked if you were Campbell."

"I heard what you said, I'm just not used people barging in to my place of work without so much as an appointment, or even the decency to introduce themselves."

"What? Oh, I'm Dolan and I want you to stop some bugger that's stealing from me. I'll give you £250 up front and another £150 if you catch them."

"Mr. Dolan, I'm not sure how you normally do business but for me it usually involves some communication, rather than demands and bluster. Now if you would like to take a seat, I'll ask you some questions and we'll have a dialogue. If that doesn't suit, you can turn around and walk back out the door." I managed to keep my voice level and calm while my blood boiled at this obnoxious excuse for a human being.

"What's the matter with you? I'm offering you good money."

"Seat or door."

"Jesus Christ." He sat down in the chair with a long drawn out huffy sigh. He was about 5 feet 5 inches tall and looked about the same around the middle. The jowls of his face almost covered the knot of his stained blue tie. What was left of his hair was already almost completely grey. Perspiration trickled on his forehead; the stale smell of tobacco and old sweat drifted over the desk. His shirt looked frayed at the collar, his brown suit had a patina of shiny overuse and a pair of off-the-shelf thick-rimmed specs completed the look of a seedy slum landlord.

"Thank you. Where did you hear about me?"

"A pal. You done some work for the insurance company he works for and he said you were all right." High praise indeed.

"Now, if theft is your problem, why haven't you gone to the police?" I enquired.

"I don't want them involved and that's all I'm telling you about that." His face took on the appearance of a sullen, stubborn child who had been asked about a broken window.

I filed that piece of information away, it appeared to me that Mr. Dolan maybe wasn't a paragon of legal virtue himself.

"OK, then I need some details before I can help, or not, as the case may be. Is it at business or personal premises that you're having the problem?"

"Business. I own a clothes factory in Lambhill. Stock is disappearing. It's happened the last two Friday nights."

"What kind of security do you have?"

"Couple of padlocks."

"No alarm, CCTV, nothing like that?"

"Not one that works, they cost cash that I've not got. There's a recession on you know."

Stupid and odious, a wonderful combination.

"What exactly would you like me to do for you?" I asked in my most patient of tones.

"Keep an eye on my place on Friday night and see if you can catch them at it. I'm sure it's an inside job, so I just want to sack them, keep the police out of it."

"OK but it'll be a flat £500 whether they turn up or not."

His face registered his shock. "What? That's daylight robbery? You'll be getting paid for no results."

"Well it won't be my fault if no one turns up and you are asking me to do a night-time surveillance. That's my fee, Mr. Dolan, it's entirely up to you." I was hoping that the money would be enough to dissuade him but it didn't work.

"All right, I suppose so." His chubby hand reached inside his suit and pulled out a cheque book and a blue Bic biro. This was a man who obviously didn't care too much about his business image. He hesitated with the pen poised above the cheque book. "How do I know you'll even turn up?"

"You don't, unless you want to sit beside me all night. You'll have to trust me."

"You better turn up or I'll sue your arse."

"And I'll sue yours if the cheque bounces," I smiled in reply, while wondering why I was doing this. Money; once again the devil had my soul.

He finished writing the cheque with an outrageous flourish of a signature and handed it over. I noticed the date on the cheque was December 16th, next Tuesday. I decided to ignore it so I could get him out of the office as soon as possible.

"I'll need some details, the address for example."

"You got a bit of paper?"

I reached over to my little ink jet printer and retrieved a blank sheet of paper. He wrote down the address and his mobile phone number.

"I'll make my report on Monday afternoon. Goodbye Mr. Dolan."

He raised his considerable bulk from the chair and turned to the door. He disappeared through it without a backward glance or a parting word.

I shook my head and put the cheque in my jeans pocket. I'm not sure how my cosy career of insurance claims had turned into murder and burglary investigations in the space of two days. It certainly was spicing up my humdrum life.

The rest of the morning was taken up with the boring admin of running my own business. I tidied up my accounts and even managed some filing to divert me from the task that lay ahead.

Around 11:30, I started to prepare myself for the meeting with Isabel. I checked my list of questions but I knew that would be more of a guideline; her answers might take me down unexpected paths. I retrieved my digital voice recorder from its drawer in the cabinet. It was an Olympus LS-10. It had been an expensive buy but the sound quality was crystal clear and when you were taking statements for an insurance report you didn't want to make a mistake because you couldn't make out what was said.

I closed up the office at 11:45 and headed for the city centre. My first interview as a proper gumshoe.

*

Royal Exchange Square sits close to the heart of the city, off Queen Street and close to the civic centre, George Square. The Gallery of Modern Art stands in the middle of the square, a Neoclassical shell housing a refurbished modern interior. Formerly the Stirling Library, the gallery opened in 1986 and its content has long divided Glaswegian opinion. It is surrounded on three sides by a collection of clubs, coffee houses, hairdressers and other boutiques to attract the more affluent citizens and visitors.

I had parked my bike in King Street car park and made my way on foot up to the café. I ordered a medium Americano and found a table close to the door. As I waited I casually glanced around at the other customers. Two middle-aged women sat with their heads bent over their table, giggling occasionally like adolescent school girls discussing the latest playground gossip. In another corner a guy who looked like a student, slouched in an armchair, a notebook computer perched precariously on his lap. Tucked away at the back of the shop were two business types; they chatted intermittently while one checked his "Blackberry" every minute for some important message that couldn't wait for him to get back to his office. If ever there was a sign of how the Western world had lost perspective on the role of work in our lives, it was the rise of mobile e-mail; a chain to ensure that you never escaped the office's clutches.

Sitting alone, close to the back of the room, was a young woman of Asian descent. She had two books in front of her, Gok Wan's 'How to look good naked' and 'What not to wear' by the television personalities Trinny Woodall and Susannah Constantine. The woman was petite but who she saw in the mirror was obviously different from the attractive person I was looking at.

I had nursed my latest caffeine fix for ten minutes before a stunning brunette approached the table.

"Mr. Campbell?" her soft Hebridean accent washed over me and she must have wondered if she was speaking to an idiot as I'm sure my jaw must have dropped.

"Eh...yes. Sorry, yes, I'm Craig Campbell."

I stood up and shook her proffered hand. She was tall and slim with striking green eyes the colour of fresh growth on a young tree. Her face was film star beautiful, with only a minimum amount of make-up to accent her best features. She wore a long brown coat that seemed to emphasise her height; a beige scarf was wrapped around her neck to protect her from the winter chill. She held a pair of mahogany-coloured leather gloves and a small matching handbag.

"Can I get you a coffee, something to eat?"

"A small latte and a piece of shortbread, please."

By the time I returned to the table she was seated, her coat draped casually over one of the spare chairs. She wore a brown business suit with a pale yellow blouse; a simple necklace with a gold heart was the only jewellery visible. The cut of the suit might have appeared severe on some women but she wore it with such natural poise and grace it only enhanced her allure.

"Thank you for agreeing to meet me," I said as I placed the coffee and shortbread on the table in front of her.

"I'm sorry if I was a bit abrupt last night. I've only just begun to get over Rory's death and your call came as quite a shock."

"I understand. Do you mind if I record our conversation?" She indicated her agreement as I took out the voice recorder from my rucksack and set it down on the table in front of us. "I need to learn more about Rory. What do you think about his mum's suspicions?"

She sipped her latte as if composing herself to answer. "I must admit I was a bit doubtful about the police version of events. Rory definitely didn't like alcohol, he was almost obsessive about it. When the police found no other evidence I began to wonder if I had misjudged him, if he had been hiding a secret from me."

"In what way was he obsessive?"

"There were one or two things. He would never let anyone buy a round of drinks without accompanying them to the bar. You know what this city is like, if you don't drink you're almost seen as a freak, a challenge to the drinkers to convert you. Rory was worried that someone would spike his orange juice but his friends always thought he was just being helpful. He also never had any drink in the flat, nothing, not for guests, not even for a dinner party. He also helped out on a Sunday night at one of the soup kitchen places for the homeless. He tried to help the people there realise what an addiction can do to their family and get them to look for help.

He was so conscious of what happened to his dad that he almost had a phobia of alcohol. He thought that the addictive personality might be hereditary."

I interrupted her train of thought, "This doesn't sound like someone who would just decide to try a drink at a Christmas night out. Do you think someone slipped him a mickey?"

"They might have, but I really don't think so. The folk in his office understood why he was the way he was. I think some of them thought it a bit weird but he was such a nice guy that no one would want to do that to him. I hope."

"How long had you two been together?"

"We'd known each other for about two years and had been going out for eighteen months. It took him six months to pluck up the courage to ask me out. We both loved art, paintings in particular. We met at the Burrell, at an exhibition of portrait painting. He was charming, a bit shy but I was attracted to him from the start. He was very handsome." She smiled despite the tears at the corners of her eyes.

"Were you living together?"

"No, he had a flat in the Merchant City, I'm in Shaw-lands. We were planning to find somewhere after Christ-mas. That was just the way he was, careful. It was nearly six months after we started to go out before we made love, he was a bit old-fashioned in that respect. He wanted everything to be just right."

"So there was no formal financial arrangement between you? No joint accounts or insurance, nothing like that?" I asked it as casually as I could.

Despite my attempt at subtlety, Isabel understood the implication behind my question, "No, Mr Campbell, there was no financial reason for me wanting Rory dead, there was no reason at all. I loved him because he was a kind, gentle soul and I wanted to share my life with him forever."

"I'm sorry, I was trying to understand the depth of your relationship. It was a clumsy, insensitive question."

"It was. But you must understand that if someone killed Rory I want them caught as much as his mum does."

"Can you think of anyone who would want to harm him? Did he have any enemies?"

"No, not at all. He loved to laugh, would do anything for anyone. He didn't go out his way to antagonise or annoy people. It just doesn't make any sense."

"Did you sense anything different about him in the lead up to his death? Anything that suggested he was anxious or depressed?"

"Well, he was a bit quieter for a couple of weeks before-hand but he said he was tired from work. There was a big tender coming up for schools in Glasgow that meant he was working long hours," she replied thoughtfully.

"Was that a regular thing, for him to be a bit different when he was busy at work?"

"Not really. He'd normally work through it even if I saw a little less of him; he was still his normal self when we were together. He wasn't very talkative in those two weeks, we would just sit and cuddle, saying very little."

"What about his work mates, was he particularly close to any of them?"

"There were a couple, Brian Swanson and Davie Stone. They shared a sense of humour and they liked the same music; they would go to gigs together."

"Do you have numbers I can contact them on?"

"Yes, I've got them here in fact." She lifted her handbag and retrieved her mobile. She gave me the numbers, which I duly recorded on my own phone.

"Have you heard much from them, since Rory's death?"

"They both called regularly immediately after his death but I suppose life moves on, I've not heard from them in a while. Davie was particularly helpful in the immediate aftermath of Rory's death. He would pop in, make a cup of tea and help me round the house. I think he did the same for Rory's mother." She let out a small sigh.

"The soup kitchent that Rory helped out at, do you know its name or where it is?"

"It was over on the south side of the river, near the Gorbals I think, but I don't know its name, or even if it has one."

"What about Rory's mum? Do you see her at all?"

"She calls once a month, as regular as clockwork. She asks how I am, I ask how she is, but that's about it. She was very protective of Rory and I don't know if at some level she blames me for his death or whether she thinks I wasn't protective enough. We used to get on well enough before his death but it's all a bit strained now." Once again the tears appeared in her eyes and this time she let them go. She cried quietly into a handkerchief as I sat watching. It's very difficult to know what to do when a beautiful stranger's grief overwhelms her, I thought an arm around her shoulder might not be appropriate.

The silent sobs stopped after about 10 minutes and she looked at her watch. "I'm sorry, I have to get back to work."

"Before you go, do you know what happened to Rory's personal effects? Did his mum take them?"

"She got most of it but I got a few things. Some photographs, his art materials, stuff like that."

"I would like to have a look at some point if that's OK."

"Sure, come over at the weekend and I'll let you see them."

We said our farewells and she headed back to her office, leaving me with my thoughts. Although I had nothing concrete, the circumstances of Rory's death were increasingly suspicious and I began to wonder why the police hadn't thought the same. I hoped that Alex might be able to fill me in on that. I packed up and walked to the bike. There wasn't much else I could do at the office today so I went straight home to try to catch up on some sleep before going to my regular Thursday quiz night at the local pub with Li and another couple of friends.

*

A bitter and biting wind was blowing from the north when I walked into the Auld Tavern. Close to Byres Road, it evokes exactly what it says on the sign. The pub dates back to the early 19th century, it still has many of the original features including a snug and sells a vast array of alcohol to suit any taste. The bar is lined with 10 hand-pumped ales, the gantry has over 60 whiskies and there is a huge selection of bottled beers and ciders from around the world.

As I passed the bar, I acknowledged Brenda, the formidable barmaid. She pointed me in the direction of Li who was sitting with our team mates Barry Fraser and Paul McCarron.

"Here's Sherlock, where have you been?" Li had his fake grumpy face on.

"Christ sake Li, I'm only 10 minutes later than usual."

"Aye but it's your round." The three comedians thrust their empty glasses at me. I removed my gloves, scarf and jacket, collected the glasses and turned towards the bar.

"Hi Brenda, the usual please."

"How's things the night, Craig?"

"Not bad. How are you?"

"Wishing I was somewhere warmer." Brenda is in her late forties, she has a strong face to match her strong character; she is respected by staff and customers alike. She was wearing a purple silk blouse over a black skirt. Her neck was draped with her collection of gold jewellery, her fingers adorned with multiple rings. She was never seen without her bling. Her face was sallow with the winter tan of a sun bed, decorated with more make-up than was needed for a pantomime. I felt that her face would be attractive enough without it but she was never seen with an unpainted face.

She worked quickly and efficiently pouring our standard round. Li's lager, Barry's Peroni, Paul's Stella and bottle of Kopparberg Pear Cider for me. Same round, every round, every week. Brenda had given up trying to persuade us to taste some of the other wonders from across the world that were available in the bar.

When I got back to the table the guys were sitting with their tongues hanging out as if they had just crossed the Sahara.

"Aye, very funny," I mumbled as I distributed the drinks from the tray.

"Li says you're a proper private dick now, at least I think that's what he said." Barry led the laughter at his own joke.

I ignored them. "Looks like it. I think there might be something there."

Li looked up. "Really? What makes you say that?"

"The picture I get of this guy is someone who was not suddenly going to go on a bender after years of being teetotal. It doesn't add up."

"Sounds heavy," Paul observed.

"I feel really sorry for his mum and his girlfriend, his mum in particular has had a lot to cope with. Hopefully Alex will be able to help."

They were just about to start asking more questions when the quiz master brought the pub to order to get the game started. As usual the tavern was packed on quiz night; our team, "Norfolk 'n' Chance" would finish in the middle order, while "Beer Goggles" and "The Frozen Few" would battle for the prize money. It was normally a great night but I was feeling more than a little distracted and wasn't much help in the first half.

When the interval came, Li wandered off to fight through the crowds at the bar.

A skinny middle-aged man approached. He was dressed in a lightweight grey jacket with polyester trousers to match and brown Hush Puppy shoes. Over his shoulder was a long black bag which still had an airport luggage tag wrapped around the handle.

"Youse lads needin' any fags?" he asked.

"No thanks, mate. We're fine," Paul replied.

"Nae worries, maybe next time eh?" The salesman walked on to the next table and asked the same question.

"Only in Glasgow would someone come direct from the airport and try to sell smuggled cigarettes to complete strangers," Paul observed.

"Can't keep a Glaswegian entrepreneur down, even in a recession," Barry said. He and Paul laughed while I managed a weak smile.

"This stuff getting to you?" Barry asked.

"Aye. It's weird, suddenly I've got something that really matters, the kind of thing that is worthwhile, and I feel completely out of my depth. I can't ask the cops to take it because I've got nothing that would count as evidence, just a feeling."

"What have you done so far?" Paul leaned forward, looking interested.

"I've spoken to Rory's mum, she was the one who came to see me, and I met his girlfriend this afternoon. I've asked Alex to have a look at the notes from the initial investigation."

Barry was also taking a keen interest. "Have you got much else to go on?"

"I've got the names of some of his colleagues from work, I'll see if they can shed any light on what happened on the night Rory died."

"What about his computer, e-mail, phone, that kind of thing?" Barry was a computer genius and it didn't surprise me that this suggestion came from him.

"That's an idea. I wonder if his mum or Isabel have kept his phone or PC for that matter."

Li returned from the bar with a tray full of drinks and crisps. "What we talking about?" he asked.

"Craig's just thinking out loud about his case," Barry replied.

"Well if there's anything we can do, mate, just let us know. Right guys?" Barry and Paul both nodded enthusiastically. It seemed that they were caught up in the thrill at the thought of being part of a murder investigation. CSI Glasgow, without the attractive women in low-cut tops. I thought that the reality of the responsibility I felt was far removed from TV's glamour.

I contributed little more to the team's efforts in the second half of the night than I did in the first. By the time the last answer had been given and the scores tallied we were a lowly third from bottom. We said our good nights and I wandered home.

Chapter Three

I woke at around 8:30 on the Friday morning. I had slept better than the night before and felt more refreshed than I had the previous day. I worked my way through my morning bathroom routine before heading to the kitchen.

I prepared porridge and put some aromatic Guatemalan coffee into the cafetiere. When I poured the hot water in, the wonderful smell permeated the kitchen in an instant and I could feel my mouth water in anticipation of the delight to come.

My kitchen is long and narrow but it suits my bachelor needs, as does the rest of my flat. It is built in the style of the majority of tenement flats across Glasgow. The ceiling is high, the bay windows at the front allow light into every crevice of the living room. There is beautiful detailing in the plaster cornicing and ceiling roses. The skirting board is a foot deep and the doors are heavy, substantial pieces of timber. I loved it and wished I could afford to buy it rather than rent; although when you see the dangers of the property market maybe I'm better off as I am.

My computer sits to the left of the bay window in my living room and I sat in front of it with my newly brewed coffee. I had decided to start my day from home rather than the office. I thought that it might be better to avoid taking on any more work; the two cases I had would take up a fair bit of time in the next week or two.

Although Rory's death was my main concern, the disagreeable Mr. Dolan would have to be considered. I launched the Firefox browser from my dock and brought up Google. When I typed Dolan's company name into the search engine the only hits on the first page were for business directories. On the second, I found a report from a local newspaper suggesting Dolan's company were being sued for wrongful dismissal but there didn't seem to be any sign of the result of the case. A disgruntled ex-employee would certainly be a possible suspect in the thefts.

I cut and pasted the details into a document that I saved to a folder on my desktop. As I was about to investigate the council tendering process, I heard my mobile phone ringing. It was still in my leather jacket from the previous evening and I got to it after 5 or 6 rings.

"Hello."

"Hi Craig, it's Alex."

"Alex, thanks for getting back to me. How did you get on?"

"I spoke to a guy that works for BTP in Port Dundas and he let me have a look at the notes from the investigation."

"What do you think?"

"I'm not sure Craig, but it does seem to have been a rushed judgement. We get so many tragic accidents around this time of year and it's easy to take things at face value."

"I'm not looking for any blame to be cast, Alex. I just want to help Mrs Kilpatrick. If I can find something tangible it might even help you guys."

"Aye, true enough. The investigation only lasted two weeks. There were some cursory interviews with Rory's mother, girlfriend and the colleagues who had attended the Christmas do. Apparently he left early, everyone seemed to think he'd had enough of his less sober colleagues. No one there thought he had been drinking, they all said that was normal for him."

"Where did the party take place?"

"One of the big hotels, the Radisson in Argyle Street."

"Pricey."

"They apparently save money every week to pay for it. Anyway, he left the hotel somewhere between 8 and 8:30. No one remembers seeing him after that."

"Why didn't the investigating officers pursue this? He lived in the Merchant City but he turns up 3 miles away from the function in the opposite direction from his home. No one saw him drinking, what did they think happened?"

Alex sounded embarrassed. "I've no idea Craig. They had already made up their mind, so they just twisted the facts to meet the theory."

"What about the post mortem?"

"There's not a lot left to post-mortem after a train hits, it's a very effective way to destroy evidence. The blood test showed about 150mg per 100ml of alcohol, that's just less than 2 times the driving limit."

"That's not dramatically high is it?"

"I wouldn't have imagined it would be enough to make him wander on a railway line. However, the officers thought that because he wasn't a regular drinker that it would have had a more dramatic effect, a view shared by the pathologist."

"Did they have any idea why he would suddenly go on a bender, with no previous history of that kind of behaviour?"

"There had been trouble at work, apparently, a couple of days before he died. No one seemed to know what it was about, it was dismissed as something trivial, his work mates felt that Kilpatrick had been stressed for a few months. One or two people suggested he had been a bit down, they thought that maybe the time of year had got to him. There was also some trouble between him and a guy called Derek Norman and something about an argument at the soup kitchen he volunteered at."

"It's not great is it?"

"No, I wouldn't be too pleased if a relative of mine died in similar circumstances and so little was done. It's not the police force's finest hour."

"Do you think they would have another look based on what you've discovered?" I asked hopefully.

"To be honest without anything more concrete I don't think so. I think you're right and there is more to this than meets the eye but the truth is we're overworked as it is and the transport boys won't want to take on any more unless they feel they can make progress quickly and with a minimum of resources. I'll do what I can." She sounded almost ashamed of her profession.

"Thanks Alex, I'll run with this and try to give you something you can use."

"Cheers, you know where I am."

When Alex rang off I dialled Mrs. Kilpatrick's number. I felt she needed to know that someone was taking her seriously.

"Hello."

"Hello, Mrs. Kilpatrick, it's Craig."

Her voice was tired and strained as she said, "Oh hello, how are you?"

"I'm fine, how are you?"

"Not good if I'm being honest."

"Mrs Kilpatrick, I've spoken to a friend of mine in the police force. She had a look at the notes from the investigation into Rory's death and unofficially she agrees with us that there is something strange about it."

"Does that mean they'll look into it?" Her voice lifted and her tone suddenly had a little bit of hope in it.

"No I'm afraid not, as I said it was unofficial but she has agreed to help where she can. If I can get some concrete physical evidence or a witness then we've got a better chance of the police pursuing this."

"Do you need more money?"

"No, no, that's not why I called. I believe you have some things of Rory's from his flat."

"That's right."

"Is there a mobile phone or a PC that I could look at?"

"There's a computer but I think he had his phone with him when he died."

"Of course. Is there any chance I can pop over and have a look tomorrow afternoon?"

"Absolutely. What time?"

"About three?"

"That's fine. I'll see you then."

"Goodbye."

Mrs Kilpatrick lived in Newlands, which was just a couple of miles from Isabel's flat in Shawlands. I would be able to visit them both tomorrow.

I felt that I was beginning to get some momentum and I wanted that to continue. I wanted to make progress so I could turn the responsibility over to the police where it belonged.

I dug out my notebook and the voice recorder from my rucksack and sat down to type up my notes. It gave me an opportunity to try to order my thoughts.

Rory was obviously traumatised by what happened to his father. Someone he had looked up to and idolised had been turned into a stranger by the effects of drink. Every indication seemed to point to him avoiding alcohol no matter what. The fact that work seemed to be preying on his mind in the run up to his death made me wonder if there was something there. Could he have had a problem with a woman at work and that's why he wouldn't tell Isabel? It was a possibility. What about the soup kitchen place? Could it be the argument he had there?

I spent the rest of the day laying out a plan on how to proceed. I would start by interviewing his two closest friends at work and expand it from there. That would give me some hint to why Rory had behaved strangely. I also had his effects to go through. Anything that troubled him may have been recorded in a diary or on his computer. Then I could visit the homeless centre and see if there was anyone there who might remember something that would help me.

Around three in the afternoon I shut the computer off and decided I needed some exercise. I changed into my running gear, plugged in my iPod and set off to pound the streets with The Fratellis playing in my ears.

My flat is within easy jogging distance of Kelvingrove Park. The park sits between Glasgow University's blackly Gothic main building and the fiery red sandstone of the Museum and Art Gallery. It is sectioned off by the river Kelvin and Kelvin Way that cuts through the heart of the area. The park was created in Victorian times as a response to the terrible urban conditions of the city. Huge trees dominate it, giving it an almost cathedral appearance when they are covered in their summer parasol of leaves. It can be a busy place on a bright summer's day but the dark chill of a winter's afternoon welcomed only the joggers and dog walkers. I ran for about 45 minutes in almost complete seclusion before turning for home.

I had a shower and a light snack before heading for my bed to get a couple hours' sleep before my night shift at Dolan's factory.

*

My alarm clock showed 8:30 pm when it noisily raised me from my brief slumber. I splashed my face with tepid water to wash the sleep away.

I dressed in three layers of warm clothing and walked through to the kitchen and put some coffee on to brew. From a lockable cabinet next to my computer in the living room I collected a pair of Canon 18X50 IS IN binoculars, my Canon EOS 5D camera with the EF 28-300 lens and a Manfrotto 682B Monopod with ball head mount. I cleaned the camera, lens and binoculars thoroughly before putting them into my camera bag. The monopod was strapped to the side. I then picked up my iPod that I had left charging and put it in the side pocket of the bag. When the coffee was brewed, I put it in a Thermos flask which also strapped on to the bag. This is my standard surveillance bag although this would be the first time I had used it at night.

I squeezed into my black bike leathers and put a reflective high-visibility vest over them. It meant I could be obvious on the way to the factory but discreet once I was there by removing the vest.

I started the bike and set off to the north side of Glasgow. The S4TS is regarded as a tourer bike, which makes it comfortable for long distances, but its Ducati heritage means it is still handles well when pushed. Mine is painted in Ducati red; a bit like a Ferrari, a Ducati should really be red. It is also, in my opinion, a cracking looking bike.

Although it was still cold, the freezing conditions of the previous week had thawed. The streets were quiet but the remains of the salt on the roads were thrown up by what traffic there was and I had to wipe the visor of my helmet to keep the dirt from obscuring my view.

Fifteen minutes after leaving my flat I was pulling into the small industrial estate off Balmore Road. Dolan's factory was near the back of the estate, close to the Forth and Clyde canal. The factory unit next to Dolan's was deserted and I pulled into the cracked and pot-holed car park. There were bushes in the corner of the car park and I parked the bike behind them so I had a good view of the entrance from the shadows while hiding the bike. I took off my helmet and the vest before taking out my iPod. I selected the "Lively" playlist that I had created to help me stay alert during surveillance duties. AC DC were first up with "Whole Lotta Rosie"; while Angus and the boys played, I attached the camera and lens to the monopod. I made myself as comfortable as I could while seated on the hard ground.

A couple of hours passed and nothing happened. At around 11:30 I noticed a set of headlights heading along the road towards me but it was only a taxi. Another hour passed, which included a cup of coffee, before another pair of headlights appeared. This time they pulled into the car park in front of Dolan's. They were the lights of a dark-coloured Peugeot Partner van. I switched on the camera and watched through the lens as it came to a stop. The driver's side of the van was closest to me so I got a good view of the young woman as she got out. She was wrapped up for the winter but I could see blonde hair falling out of her woollen hat. I was expecting someone else to exit at the passenger door but she was alone. I photographed as much as I could, the camera already set for ISO 3200 to allow me to capture as much detail as possible in the dark conditions.

I watched her walk round the van to the door of the factory. She put her hands into her coat pocket and retrieved a set of keys. There appeared to be two padlocks as well as a lock on the door itself. After opening all three she stepped through the door. She was out of sight for about ten minutes before she reappeared with two black refuse bags, obviously filled with something. I shot a few more photographs and began to pack the camera away as I was worried she would drive away before I could follow her. I needn't have worried; after she had thrown the bags into the back of the van through a side door just behind the driver's door, she walked back into the factory. She was only gone a few seconds when she emerged with another two bags and put them beside the others. She then closed the van door, turned back to the factory door and locked everything she had opened.

When she was back in the driver's seat of the van I packed up the rest of my kit, put my helmet on and was ready to follow her on the bike. She drove the van round in a large circle and out of the car park. I allowed her a slight lead before pulling the bike on to the road. I watched from a distance as she turned left on the way out of the industrial estate and then I put a little pace into the bike to ensure I didn't lose her at the first set of lights. When I turned on to Balmore Road she was sitting at the lights waiting for the red to turn green. Another car was between us and that suited me fine. I had noticed previously that following someone on a bike was easier as most drivers didn't see bikers at all, we were virtually invisible on our two-wheeled machines.

I followed at a safe distance all the way down Balmore Road and on to Saracen Street. She turned on to Possil Road and I continued to track her all the way to the Clydeside Expressway that headed west beside the river. She drove for a few miles before turning off beyond Partick at the housing development called Glasgow Harbour. I was surprised as this was an expensive part of town, overlooking the water. The apartments had fantastic views across the south of the city and along the Clyde itself. They stood on a site that once was dominated by an enormous grain store and were part of the regeneration of Glasgow's waterfront that had begun over twenty years earlier.

The van pulled up outside a block of flats positioned on the waterfront. They were the first blocks to sell out despite being the most expensive. My thief was living more like Raffles than Bill Sykes. I rode past the entrance and parked the bike about 100 yards away. I watched as she took the first two bags into the foyer; it didn't look like she was a visitor. While she was inside I walked nearer to the entrance and when she came back out for the other bags I said, "Excuse me."

She jumped with surprise.

"Sorry, I didn't mean to startle you, but I've got some questions for you."

She was obviously defensive and moved to put the van between us. "Who are you? What do you want?"

"My name's Craig Campbell and I was hired by your employer to find out who was stealing from him."

"My employer?" She looked perplexed.

"Yes, Mr. Dolan."

"Oh Christ, he's not my employer."

"What?" It was my turn to feel puzzled.

"He's my uncle. You'd better come in. Give me a hand with these bags." This wasn't quite going as I had thought it might.

I picked up both bags, which probably made me an accessory after the fact. I followed her into the inviting and well-lit lobby. The other bags were lying beside the lift door and she pressed the button. We stood for a few seconds in awkward silence before it arrived to carry us to the fourth floor. We turned to the right where she opened her apartment door.

"Put the bags down in the hall, the living room is straight ahead."

I did as commanded and found myself with a spectacular view across Glasgow. The lights of the city gleamed with added sparkle as Christmas decorations added to the usual phosphorescence. The room was furnished in IKEA modern and looked comfortably warm in a range of brown tones.

"Sorry, I didn't introduce myself, I'm Carol Parker," she said as she walked into the room behind me. I turned and shook her hand. She had removed her outdoor clothing and I found myself looking at an extremely attractive girl. She was in her early twenties, petite with shoulder length blonde hair and bright blue eyes that sparkled behind trendy designer spectacles. She was dressed in a red fleecy jumper and dark jeans.

"Hi Carol. I'm Craig Campbell."

"Sit down, do you fancy a tea or a coffee?"

"Coffee, please."

"Espresso, cappuccino, filtered, instant?"

"Instant will be fine, thanks." I was still drifting along not sure how I had lost control of the situation, it had even affected my choice of coffee.

She pottered about in the kitchen that was separated from the living room by a breakfast bar that doubled as a cupboard. I watched her from my vantage point on a comfortable, red leather chair. She moved with a simple economy of effort that was pleasing on the eye. She placed a jug of milk and a sugar bowl on the table in front of me. The coffee made, she walked into the living room and sat down on a two-seater couch which was wrapped in the same leather as my chair.

"So are you some kind of private eye or something?" she asked as she handed me my coffee.

"Insurance investigator officially, although I seem to be having an involuntary change of job title this week." I splashed some milk into my mug.

She smiled as she said, "Uncle John got you sleuthing for him to find his terrible thief? He's a cracker isn't he?"

"He's an interesting character." I tried to keep my voice as neutral as I could.

"It's OK, I know he's an ogre, or is that an insult to ogres?" Her smile was warm and genuine.

"He didn't make a very good impression, I'm not sure he was too enamoured when I stood up for myself." It was my turn to smile.

"He knows that I'm the one taking the clothes," she said. "He just wants to try to teach me a lesson."

My surprise must have shown on my face as I replied,"Oh, he doesn't seem the type to spend £500 for something he doesn't need."

"He won't, he'll take it out of my salary. He's as tight as a duck's you know what."

"Aye, he came across as warm and cuddly as Scrooge before the ghosts paid him a visit."

"Do you want to hear the story of my life with my kindly old Uncle Scrooge?" she asked.

"Go on then."

"My Mum died when I was born, I never knew my Dad. My Aunt Alice is my mother's sister and she's the poor unfortunate that's married to Uncle John; she took me in and I was raised by them as if I were their daughter. Auntie Alice is fantastic, full of fun and very loving, I couldn't have asked for more. Despite appearances Uncle John isn't a grumpy old sod all the time and he took an interest in me when I was growing up. When I was very young he would read me stories, he would ask me about my progress at school, go to parent nights and functions. He's just not very good at the emotional bit, like aw you West of Scotland men." There was a heavy emphasis on the last part of the sentence.

She sipped her coffee.

"He's changed a lot in the last five years or so, particularly where the business is concerned. He had a partner who buggered off with a large chunk of the company's cash, leaving it in a precarious position. Uncle John had to borrow from the bank to stay afloat. He always ran the business with a healthy cash surplus to allow him to buy machinery or whatever without having to be in hock to the bank."

"How long have you worked there?"

"About 3 years, ever since I finished Uni basically."

"What about the thefts? You don't look like someone who needs to be nicking stuff from your employer."

"The stuff we produce is pretty high end and they need to be made to exacting standards. The smallest of faults in the stitching, the material or the cut will see them rejected by the stores we supply. I collect the rejects once a week and give them to a charity that supports orphanages and hospitals in Romania, Bulgaria and Albania. It's just my way of giving something back."

"Does your Uncle know?"

"Where the clothes are going, you mean?"

I nodded.

"Probably. I only started doing it when he refused to allow me to do it officially."

His reasoning suddenly dawned on me. "That's why he involved me rather than the police, I thought he was up to something dodgy."

"Aye, it's all just an effort to teach me a lesson about how business works. It's a shame that he's like this now, the only thing he takes any interest in is the business and his chihuahuas."

I laughed, "Chihuahuas?"

"He breeds and shows them, they're his new babies. You should see him prancing round the show ring with one of his precious pups at the end of a lead."

She giggled in a charming and infectious way and I found myself attracted to this interesting girl.

"What happens next? Are you going to slap the cuffs on me, copper?" she asked lightly.

"It's not my scene but if it's what you're into."

"Oi, you know what I meant," she said in mock anger at my less than subtle flirting.

"I've to report back to grumpy on Monday."

"Come to the factory early in the morning and I'll help you deliver the shocking news."

"Right, that should be an interesting meeting. I better head. Thanks for the coffee." I stood up and walked to the front door with Carol behind me.

"Nice meeting you, Craig."

"You too." We shook hands again and I walked to the lift. I turned to look back and she was still standing at the door. We waved as I stepped through the doors.

On the short journey home I reflected on a bizarre conclusion to my first criminal surveillance. Flirting with an alluring girl wasn't quite how I'd expected it to end, but I was very pleased that it had.

Chapter Four

After a few hours sleep, I set off for the south side of Glasgow at around midday on the Saturday.

Mrs. Kilpatrick lived in Carvalerock Road, part of a Victorian suburb with substantial red and blonde sandstone villas. Her house was set back from the road with a small drive leading up to the pillared entrance. I parked the bike in front of a brick built garage to the right of the front door. I pressed the doorbell and somewhere in the house a small dog started barking and raced to beat Mrs. Campbell to the door.

Anne greeted me with a small smile, "Hello, Mr. Campbell." The dog was a West Highland Terrier and he bounced excitedly around me as I crossed the threshold.

"Don't worry about Angus, he's a softy," she said as she escorted me through a small hall in to an airy front room. It was decorated in simple style with dark oak furniture that looked to be about the same age as the house. There was a sideboard, a couple of bookcases in alcoves and a coffee table. On each side of the table were two chesterfield style settees, covered in a dark green, aged leather. The enormous windows were decorated with velvet curtains in a similar colour to the sofas and the walls complemented them in a pale but warm green. There was also a wooden fireplace with carved Charles Rennie Mackintosh style roses, ceramic tiles decorated both sides; family photographs adorned the mantel and on the walls there was a collection of still life paintings.

She sat on the settee nearest the window and indicated the other one, "Have a seat."

After I had made a fuss of Angus he made himself comfortable in front of the fireplace.

"How are you?" I asked.

"I'm a little better after to speaking to you last night, I think I came to the right man." She wrung her hands in a nervous gesture I had noticed when we first met.

"I hope you're right but I will tell you that I will do my utmost to move this forward for you, at least to the point where I can hand it over to the professionals."

"What can I do for you today?"

"I'd like to have a look at Rory's effects to see if there is anything there that might help me."

"I put everything I wanted to keep up in his old room; come up and you can have a look."

We headed back into the hall and up the curved staircase, along a short hall to the room at the front of the house with Angus trotting obediently behind. The room was about half full of boxes, a jumble of sizes, colours and shapes. Close to the window there was a PC, sitting on a desk made of brushed chrome and pale green frosted glass.

"What's in the boxes?"

"His books, some of his sketch books and small paintings. I gave his clothes, music and DVDs to a charity shop but I couldn't bear to part with the more personal things."

"Is the computer Rory's?"

"Yes. I don't know why I didn't get rid of that, it sits there all the time and I never turn it on."

"Would it be OK if I have a look?"

"Of course, of course. Do you want a drink or something to eat?"

"I'd love a coffee."

She disappeared downstairs and I sat myself down in front of the PC. It wasn't connected up so I collected the necessary peripherals and plugged them into their respective sockets. It was a pretty standard HP consumer machine and it wasn't long before the fan was whirring as it began its boot up process. I had long ago abandoned Windows as my operating system but knew my way around the XP Home Edition that the machine was running. Rory hadn't bothered with a password and after the virus checker had popped up to tell me it was out of date, the boot up sequence finally settled to the default desktop; a picture of Rory and Isabel on a beach somewhere. They looked relaxed and happy in each other's company.

Mrs Kilpatrick returned with the coffee and hovered at the door while I searched the computer for some detail that might help.

I navigated the menu system and clicked on Internet Explorer to check the history. There were the usual collection of shopping sites, utilities and news sites that most people have. There was also a few dedicated to art and one or two for sport. There were two that caught my eye; a site for a self-storage firm and a company called New Future Homes. I then browsed through the My Documents and My Pictures folders but there was nothing of note. I loaded Outlook Express and checked his e-mail. I noticed an invoice from the same self storage company, dated two days before Rory died. I took note of the details of the storage unit's address in my ever trusty notepad.

"Mrs Kilpatrick, did you find a key among Rory's things, one you didn't recognise maybe?"

She paused before saying, "I don't think so. I gave his flat keys back to the landlord after I cleared the flat and there were a couple of keys that looked like they were for a desk or a filing cabinet so I sent them to his office."

"That's fine, I'll speak to Isabel when I see her later, she might have found something."

I continue to search the computer for anything else that might help but it was fairly dull humdrum stuff, music, household letters and photographs. I shut down the machine and we went back downstairs.

"Did it help?" Mrs Kilpatrick asked.

"Well, maybe. Rory rented a storage unit just before he died; it's possible he stored something that might give us a clue as to why he was murdered."

"Thank you for everything you're doing. Are you sure you don't need any money?"

"I'm fine at the moment. I'm going to pop off to see Isabel and I'll keep you up to date with any progress I make."

I motioned to shake her hand but she stepped in and gave me a hesitant hug.

"Thank you for taking me seriously."

I hugged her in return and walked to the bike.

*

Isabel's flat is a five minute bike ride from the Kilpatrick house, in Tantallon Road. The area is a mirror for my own part of Glasgow; the same red sandstone tenements dominate with all of the same parking problems. Kilmarnock Road is the main thoroughfare and like Byres Road in the West End it is a haven of delicatessen, fancy eateries and pubs. It is almost as if the students of Glasgow University on graduation, migrate south of the river and live in their own professional ghetto. Although it is changing these days as the Merchant City and riverside developments lay a claim on those same graduates.

After about ten minutes touring the surrounding area I found a space for the bike and then had a walk to get to Isabel's close. I rang the buzzer for her flat on the controlled entry panel to the right of the main door.

"Hello?" Isabel's voice was almost masked due to the tinny sound of the speaker.

My voice was probably too loud in reply as I said, "Isabel, it's Craig Campbell."

"OK."

The buzzer sounded, indicating that the door was open. Isabel lived on the third floor so I had plenty of time to admire the beautiful tiles that lined the stairwell. It is sad to think how many of these buildings were knocked down in the sixties and seventies in Glasgow's mad rush to modernise it's architecture. The square, characterless tower blocks that had replaced them were now being torn down themselves, the evidence of an architectural and social experiment that went wrong is being erased.

I was slightly out of breath when I reached Isabel's door just as it swung open.

"Hi Craig, in you come."

The flat was laid out in a mirror image of my own as it was on the opposite side of the close. I walked through the hall into the spacious living room. It was tastefully decorated in subtle tones of lilac and purple. The furniture was simple, ornamentation was minimal; Isabel had managed to make it look modern without being obtrusive on the Victorian style of the building itself. On the main wall above a white fireplace was a portrait of Isabel that I guessed was painted by Rory; it was a beautifully natural picture, Isabel smiling with her head tilted slightly to one side, her hair cascading down to frame her face.

"He was very talented wasn't he?" Isabel had noticed me admiring the picture.

"He was indeed."

"How are you getting on with the investigation?"

I gave her a brief summary of the current information, of Alex's opinion that there was probably something worth pursuing. I asked her about the storage unit but she didn't know any more than Mrs. Kilpatrick.

"I'll get Rory's things."

She left the room and I looked around. The alcove to the left of the fireplace had been converted into a bookshelf and it was populated with some large art books, classic fiction and one or two biographies. Apart from the portrait there were no other family pictures on display other than a small photograph of Rory hamming it up for the camera.

Isabel returned with a large packing case. "This is everything I wanted."

She placed the box in front of me and I began to look through the contents. I flicked through several sketch books; Rory's talent was again obvious as I scanned a variety of subject matter including animals, landscapes, portraiture and still life. I realised that the paintings in Mrs. Kilpatrick's living room were developed from some of the sketches I was looking at. Below the sketch books were small oil studies, again a reference for working up bigger canvases. There were a collection of photo albums, Isabel and Rory on holiday, at Christmas and days out. I looked at the happy faces of two people obviously in love and enjoying sharing their lives, the sadness of the situation Isabel now found herself in touched me. Both of the women in this young man's life had their hearts broken by what appeared to be a totally baffling attack.

At the very bottom of the case was a wooden multi-tiered artist box, the layers beneath were revealed as I opened the top tier. Rory was tidy and everything was organised neatly in the box; there was a range of oil paints, fine quality brushes made of hog's hair, charcoal pencils, paint solvents, cloths for cleaning the brushes and a variety of erasers. I inspected each tier carefully and at the very bottom beneath the cloths I found a key.

"Isabel, do you recognise this?" I held up the key for her to see.

She reached for it and I passed it to her. She scrutinised it but I could tell from her face that it wasn't ringing any bells in her memory.

"No, I'm afraid not. Do you think that could be the storage key?"

"I hope so. Would it be OK if I take it with me?"

"Of course."

I packed the crate again and Isabel took it away. I gathered my helmet and I was ready to leave when she came back into the room.

"Thanks for that Isabel, I hope it wasn't too painful."

"That's OK. I just hope it will help."

"There's a couple of things I'd like to find out. I asked you if Rory had any enemies but I was wondering if there was an old boyfriend in your past that might have resented Rory, been jealous enough to harm him."

"Not in Glasgow, Rory was the first guy I went out with down here."

"What about from home?"

"I can't imagine so."

"Was there anybody in his circle of friends or acquaintances that behaved inappropriately towards you?"

"Well, I wouldn't say inappropriate but there was this one guy from his work. Anytime we were in his company he would follow me, stand next to me. It was a little weird. Derek Norman was his name. Rory's friends called him "Norman No Mates", Rory reckoned he was a bit shy and didn't know how to socialise with men or women."

"Did he work in the same office as Rory?"

"No, I think he was in accounts or something financial."

"OK thanks, I'll see if anyone can help me with a phone number and I'll have a word with him."

"Do you think it could be him?"

"People can become obsessive sometimes and they can see things that aren't really there. It could be that this Norman character saw Rory as an obstacle to his fantasy of being with you. It's just a theory."

"I understand."

We said our goodbyes and I headed for home through the Christmas shopping traffic. I managed to remain focused on the road, while my mind raced with the possibilities of who had done what and why.

Chapter Five

The following morning I decided to try and get hold of Rory's mates but first the domestic chores had to be done. I vacuumed and dusted the flat, put on my washing, prepared and ate my breakfast all before I headed to Li's flat at ten.

The only problem with my bike was that it wasn't much use when it came to carrying shopping, so Li and I had come to an agreement that he would take me for my weekly shop every Sunday morning in return for my giving him a lift home during the working week.

I locked up and went down to Mrs. Capaldi's door; I always liked to check if she needed anything when we were going to the shop anyway.

"Well if it's no ma favourite handsome neighbour," she said upon opening the door.

"Hi Mrs. C. You need anything from the supermarket this week?"

"Could ye get me some butter, none o' that spreadable rubbish a proper pack of butter, mind?"

"I remember. Anything else?"

"Oh I need some extra virgin olive oil as well."

"OK, no problem."

"And get yourself a wee sweetie for going," she tousled my hair as she laughed at another of our regular bits of banter.

"Are you off to church?"

"Ah don't think I'll bother this week, son, it's too cold."

"Catch you later."

"Ciao."

I walked the short distance to Li's flat where he was waiting for me.

"Morning Craig"

"Hi Li, how's things?"

"Busy. I was rushed off my feet yesterday, everybody wanting their Christmas haircut."

"It pays the bills, mate."

We got in to his slightly creaky white Honda Civic, I cleared the usual detritus of parking tickets and chocolate wrappers from the seat before adjusting it into position.

"When are you ever going to clear this skip?" I said with as much disgust as I could muster.

Li's broad grin never flinched as he replied, "Chill out man. It's on one of my to do lists."

On the way to the supermarket in Maryhill Road he asked about my "big case" as he called it. I filled him in on the details of what had been done so far and what else there was still to do. One of the reasons I like Li is he never seems to have a negative thought; his comments were entirely positive, reassuring me that I was going in the right direction, that the information I needed was just round the corner and that I would be doing a good thing for Mrs. Kilpatrick and Isabel.

We wandered around the store like the experienced grocery shoppers we were; we noticed price increases, new deals, discussed the merits of Persil washing powder over Daz. Our rock 'n' roll lifestyle never stops.

Li drove home and I carried the shopping into the flat, dropping Mrs. Capaldi's butter and oil off on the way up. I unpacked the bags and put a new Guatemalan blend on to brew, a treat to myself that I had purchased that morning.

When the coffee was ready, I settled into the couch in the living room with the phone, the ever present notepad and pen poised. I flicked through the pad and found the numbers that Isabel gave me for Brian Swanson and Davie Stone. I dialed Brian's number, the phone responded with a number unavailable tone. Thinking that I had misdialled, I tried again being careful with each number I pressed but the result was the same. As it was a mobile number, I presumed that Brian had changed his service or maybe had bought a new phone.

My luck changed with Davie Stone's number, it rang immediately and a voice answered after three rings, "Hello." The voice was male and hesitant, obviously puzzled by the unfamiliar number.

"Hi, is that Davie Stone?"

"Yes. Who's this?"

"My name's Craig Campbell, I'm investigating the death of a friend of yours, Rory Kilpatrick."

"Investigating? Are you a cop?"

"No I'm a private investigator." It sounded strange even to me.

"I thought they only existed in books and films," he replied with more than a degree of scepticism.

"Mrs. Kilpatrick has asked me to have a look into Rory's death."

"It was an accident, wasn't it?"

"Well it's beginning to look like there's more to it. I was hoping you could help me."

"I don't how much help I'll be but anything you need, it's no problem. Rory was a top bloke."

"Can I come to see you?"

"Aye, come over this afternoon if you want."

He gave me his address and I arranged to visit around two that afternoon.

I placed the phone back in the cradle feeling a bit more positive as avenues of investigation opened up for me.

I prepared myself for a run around Kelvingrove Park to help me think it through; I was now more determined than ever to get to the bottom of this.

*

I arrived at Davie Stone's house around five to two. He lived in the flat on the top floor at the left side of a four in a block style building. The houses were originally built by Glasgow Corporation but many of them were now owner occupied.

I walked up the narrow path to the door which was on

the side of the building. The door bell chimed and a short while later it was opened by a small, balding man in his mid to late thirties.

"Craig?" he asked.

"That's me, I take it you are Davie?"

"Aye, in you come."

He showed me into the internal stairway that led me up into the flat itself. The walls were painted white and there was no carpet on the concrete steps. As I walked up, the smell of tobacco smoke grew stronger with every step. Ever since the ban on smoking in public places my senses seemed to have intensified to the pungent and acrid aroma of cigarettes. I felt myself almost gag at the strength of this particular brand.

"Straight along the hall to the room at the end," he advised me when I reached the top of the staircase

I walked along the length of the hall and could see a blue haze through the open door of, what I presumed, was the living room. It was all I could do not to cough as I walked into the smoke filled space. The walls were brown with nicotine and looked like they hadn't been decorated since the seventies. The wallpaper was patterned with large gold and green flowers, the colours were faded and covered in a sepia coating produced by years of tobacco smoke. On one wall stood a large teak unit, with smoked glass doors on the top and a set of drawers at the bottom. The shelves behind the doors held a number of family photographs, including the picture of a man in naval uniform. One shelf was dedicated to a series of plates commemorating royal events, the Coronation of Queen Elizabeth, the marriage of the Queen and Prince Philip, a variety of birthdays and in pride of place a delicate china plate depicting the marriage of Prince Charles and Lady Diana Spencer. The carpet dated from the same period as the rest of the decor, in places there were marks where ash had fallen, flicked carelessly at an ashtray.

"Who is it, David?" asked a diminutive woman sitting in an armchair beside the fireplace.

"Just a man to ask about Rory, mum" he replied.

"Oh that poor lad, it was terrible what happened to that boy." She took a long draw on a half-smoked cigarette and added to the fog in the room. By the look of the ashtray next to her it wasn't her first of the day, not even the twenty-first.

"Craig Campbell, this is my mother, Agnes."

"Pleased to meet you, Mrs Stone." It was only as I bent to offer my hand that I noticed that she was blind. I moved my hand to hers and shook it gently.

"Would you let me feel your face, son?"

"Mum!" Her son exclaimed.

"No, that's OK." She rested her cigarette on the edge of the ashtray. I leaned further forward and placed her hands on my face. She ran her hands over every feature, the smell of nicotine filled my nostrils with even greater potency.

"Ah, that's a good honest face if ever I felt one." She laughed but it caught in her throat and she coughed, a hacking sound that I imagined was painful. She reached for a glass on the table at her right hand and drank some kind of fruit drink. When she was finished she lifted the cigarette and took another deep draw.

"Do you want a cup of tea, Mr. Campbell?" Davie offered.

"Please, call me Craig. Coffee if you've got it."

"No problem, Craig, what do you take?"

"Just a spot of milk, please"

"Do you want a cuppa, Mum?"

"Aye ye know me, never say no to a cuppa."

I was still standing and Mrs Stone realised it, "Sit down son, you'll make the place look untidy."

I sat on a three-seater leather sofa that matched the two armchairs in the room.

"So what is you do, Craig?"

"Well normally I do investigations for insurance companies but at the moment I'm doing some detective work."

"About that boy's death? That was terrible, I keep thinking about his poor mother. I don't know what I would do without my David."

"Does David have brothers or sisters?"

"Aye, one brother. He's in London working in some fancy hotel but he never bothers wi' us. He's married to this stuck up woman and she doesn't want anything to do with her Scottish relations. It's just been David and I since he went south in 1990."

"Is the man in the Navy uniform their Dad?"

"That's him, Andy. He died in the Falklands in 1982 when Davie was just ten. His brother was 9. I lost my sight in 1989 and David's had to look after me ever since."

"It must have been hard for you both."

"It's not been easy on him, but he's been good to me."

Davie returned with the drinks on a tray that commemorated the investiture of the Prince of Wales in 1969. On the tray there were three mugs and a plate of biscuits. Davie placed his mother's tea on her table, "Do you want a biscuit?"

"I'll have a caramel wafer."

He handed her the snack and then offered me the plate. I took a biscuit, unwrapped it and then lifted my coffee.

"What do you want to know, Craig?" Davie asked after he had settle in the other armchair opposite his mother.

"Do you mind if I record this?"

"No, go ahead."

I lifted my recorder from a pocket in my leathers, switched it on and placed it on the coffee table in the centre of the room.

"Well, I would like to know about Rory and to see if there is anything you can tell me that might give me a clue as to who killed him, if he was murdered."

"Me and Rory were good mates. We met in the office and got to chatting, as you do. I think the fact that we had both lost our fathers when we were young gave us a bond. We had a similar taste in music, we would go to the occasional gig together, socialise away from work every now and again, that kind of thing."

"What did you think about his attitude to alcohol?"

"At first it was a bit strange, he was so obsessive about it but he was never preachy, he never tried to tell any of his friends or folk from the office not to drink. After a while we would joke about it but I think everybody respected his views."

"Do you think anyone would have slipped him something at the Christmas do? Thinking it was a bit of a laugh"

"I don't think so, I would hope not." He sounded convinced.

"Can you remember much of what happened that night?"

"We finished work about one that afternoon, the meal was booked for two. Rory, Brian, Audrey, Joe and I walked down to the hotel together. A few others were already there when we got there and the rest arrived in drips and drabs. We had a nice meal and then there was a dance after. The DJ must have started about five, I think. There was a big crowd of people as there were four or five of the offices booked for the meal. Everyone was circulating, speaking to people they hardly talk to all year. I chatted to Rory twice maybe three times but he loved to dance and of course looking like he did there were plenty of willing partners. The majority in the hall were pretty drunk by about eight, I believe that was the last time I saw Rory."

He paused as the memory was painful for him, he swallowed hard before continuing, "I went looking for him about ten as I was heading home but someone said he had already left."

"Do you remember him arguing with someone either that night or in the lead up to it?"

"No, nothing like that. He had to talk to a guy in procurement, Derek Norman, about a week before. Someone told him that Derek had a picture of Rory's girlfriend, Isabel, on his phone. I'm not sure what was said but Rory wasn't the type to go storming in."

"What do you think of Derek Norman?"

"He's a bit of a loner, the women in the office don't like him, they say he's a bit creepy."

"In what way?"

"They say he invades their personal space, not touching or anything but just standing closer than they feel comfortable with. I'm not sure, he just seems to lack any sense of proper boundaries. He also has really bad B.O. and I think that puts the girls off more than anything else."

"Is there any other details you can remember about that time? Was there some kind of trouble with work?"

"Rory always got a bit more withdrawn when he was under pressure. The two weeks running up to the Christmas break were manic, we had to complete the bidding process and ensure everything was ready to put to the committee. Rory was a perfectionist and if he felt something wasn't right he would tell the bosses in no uncertain terms, sometimes they listened but when we were under that kind of pressure I think they just told him to keep his opinions to himself. I'm sure that was the case that week."

"Was Rory the type to have a fling? You said he was popular with the women in the office."

"No way, Rory was definitely a one woman man. He loved Isabel. He was very committed to her and he spoke about them moving into a flat together and eventually getting married."

"OK. Do you have any contact numbers for Brian Swanson, I'm not getting an answer from the number Isabel gave me?"

He looked a bit sheepish as he said, "I'm afraid Brian's dead."

"Oh. What happened?"

"He was killed in June, it was a car accident. He lost control of the car on a sharp bend on a country road, driving to his brother's house in Aberfoyle. The car hit a tree and he was killed instantly."

"Was there any suggestion of alcohol playing a part?"

"No, at least not as far as I know."

"Why didn't you let Isabel know?"

"I couldn't bring myself to do it. I knew it would bring back bad memories for her, I just didn't have the courage to tell her so I stopped calling."

"Oh son, how could you do that to her?" interjected Mrs. Stone.

"Tell her I'm sorry if you see her. It's hard dealing with other people's grief."

"I know." I reached forward and stopped the recorder.

"Thanks for your help with this, Davie. I know it can't be easy for you."

"No problem, if you need anything else just let me know."

"Oh there is one thing, Derek Norman. I don't suppose you have a number for him do you?"

"I do as a matter of fact, he came along to a bowling night we had and he called me for directions. I store the numbers of anyone who rings me, just in case they come in handy for something."

"Can you send it to my phone, please?"

"Will do." He left the room and returned with his mobile. A couple of seconds later my phone beeped as his message arrived.

"Thanks for that. I'll leave you my card and you can get in touch if you think of anything else. Bye, Mrs Stone." I handed Davie the card.

"Bye, son. Nice meeting you." The old lady waved as I walked out of the room. Davie escorted me to the outside door and we shook hands before I walked back to the bike.

*

I rode the bike to a fast food outlet at Parkhead Forge and grabbed a late unhealthy lunch. As I sat in the faux American diner, I decided to try and get a hold of Mr. Norman. As the police say, he was certainly a person of interest in connection with this case. It looked like he had a problem relating to women and that can sometimes lead to a distorted view of reality.

I found his name in my address book and pressed to dial.

"Hello, Derek Norman speaking." There was a hint of Geordie accent in the soft spoken voice.

"Hi, my name is Craig Campbell. I was wondering if I could have a chat with you about Rory Kilpatrick."

"Who?"

"Craig Campbell, I'm an insurance investigator."

"What do you want to talk to me about?"

I decided to try a different approach as he seemed to be very guarded. "I'm looking into Rory Kilpatrick's death, there seems to be some doubt that his death was an accident. As you may know insurance policies don't pay out on suicide and we have had some suggestion that he may have taken his own life."

"Well, I hardly knew him. I can't see me being much help."

"I'm trying to get a picture of his mental state, so I'm interviewing as many people as I can who came into contact with him."

"OK then."

"Are you free this afternoon?"

"Come round about six, I'll talk to you then."

"That's fine, thanks very much. Where do you live?"

He gave me his address before hanging up. I checked my watch, it was three-thirty. I decided to go back to the flat for a couple of hours before going to meet him. He had sounded cautious and more than a little hesitant about talking to me. It would be an interesting meeting.

*

Norman's flat was in a high rise building at the corner of Garscube Road and St. George's Road. I took the lift to the fourth floor and found the apartment number he had given me. I rattled the letter box and the door was opened.

I wasn't sure what I was expecting but it wasn't the towering mountain of muscle that stood in front of me.

"Hi, I'm Craig Campbell, I called earlier."

"Come in." I followed him through a short hallway into the living room. The room was painted completely white, a pair of mocha coloured curtains hung limply at the window, the floor was covered in a pale wood laminate. There were only two chairs, both covered in a plain blue fabric The only other furniture was an old television, nothing else occupied any floor space. There were no pictures on the wall, nothing that would give anyone a clue as to the character of the person living there. The atmosphere was filled with the smell of a floral air freshener which didn't quite cover the smell of bitter sweat, that I thought would indicate a glandular rather than a cleanliness problem.

He indicated one of the seats and I sat down as ordered. He remained standing, his considerable bulk filling the room and adding a slightly intimidating air. I guessed he was around 35 years-old, his hair was cropped close to his head, his face was red and very pockmarked as if he had very bad acne as a teenager. He had cool blue, almost grey eyes that stared intently at me while his hands busied themselves in front of his body; they never stopped moving during the course of our conversation. He was dressed in a tight, pale orange t-shirt and a pair of black athletic trousers, on his feet were a pair of expensive looking trainers.

"What is it you need from me Mr. Campbell?"

"I've got one or two questions regarding Rory Kilpatrick. I believe you worked with him."

"Not with him, no. I'm in procurement, I had to contact him about certain bits of work." The hesitancy I had noticed on the phone was still very much in evidence.

"What kind of work?"

"There were times when we had to go to the same meetings; there's some slight overlap between his role and mine but that was all."

"What was your impression of him?"

"He was quiet, shy but seemed to be good at his job."

"Did you ever socialise with him?"

"Not really, other than an office night out. I'm not one for drinking, we had that in common." He smiled in a strange way, as if his face didn't get much practice.

"Was he popular in the office?"

"I suppose so."

"Was there ever any trouble between you?"

His stare became even more intense as the creepy smile was replaced with a hint of anger.

"There was a misunderstanding but I don't see what it's got to do with you or any insurance company. I think maybe it's time for you to leave Mr. Campbell, if that's really your name."

"Do you mean the incident with the phone?"

He stepped towards me and grabbed my arm, his face was set in a vicious snarl as he hauled me to my feet and pushed me in the direction of the door. "I said it's time for you to leave."

"If it was a misunderstanding, why are you so unwilling to talk about it?" I asked, pushing my luck.

"Get oot." He shouted, his accent was now more pronounced.

I didn't feel capable of overcoming him in a physical confrontation, so I walked to the door of the flat. He slammed the door behind me without another word. I could understand why he was treated with suspicion by the people in his workplace. His sudden burst of anger made me want to know more about him. More digging was necessary.

*

Although it had been a busy day my work wasn't over. Rory had helped out on a Sunday at a soup kitchen in the Gorbals, close to the southern bank of the Clyde. I had resolved to go there that night to see if I could get some information about the argument that Alex had mentioned.

After a quick dinner, I spent the evening in the flat at my computer, tidying up my accounts for submission in January. I wasn't very successful as my thoughts kept drifting to Derek Norman. My encounter with him had given me a lot to think about and I wondered how I could get more information on him. He wasn't a native to the city and it looked like he hadn't made a very good impression on people since he arrived. It was a problem for another day.

Around 10 o'clock, I made my way into the city centre, the roads were nearly empty, deserted in the quiescent Sunday night. The streets glittered as the Christmas lights were reflected by the rain polished tarmac.

The building was an old red sandstone structure, I wasn't sure whether it was an old civic or church hall but it was obviously not in the best of repair. The rain water cascaded down from a blocked or broken gutter, the windows were spider-webbed with cracks, the paint was peeling, the stonework was chipped and worn. A dim light shone through the craquelere effect of the windows.

I walked round to the entrance, there were a couple of crumbling steps up into the building, a pair of Corinthian pillars guarded the portal, the detail eroded away by too many Scottish winters. The heavy, dark wooden doors were opened into a small vestibule. There were two doors into the main room, I walked to the left and entered the hall. The air smelled of broth and beer, precipitation and perspiration, dirt and damp.

A row of tables split the hall into two halves; in each half there were several small groups of men huddled around portable gas fires. It looked almost Dickensian, the dim light, the figures dressed in torn clothes with their faces illuminated by the fire as they gathered, stretching out to the heat and conversing in hushed tones. At the far end was a stage, tattered velvet curtains hung like the faded rags of an actress who had fallen on hard times. In front of the stage was a table, there were plates, cutlery and bread arranged on it. Beside the table there were two urns balanced precariously on a catering trolley.

A young man rose from one of the groups and walked towards me. He was in his late twenties, slim and dressed in a blue casual shirt with jeans. The neck of the shirt was open and I could see a small wooden cross resting against the top of his breast bone. His hair was coal black and thick, he had an olive complexion, a genuine smile curled his lips and reached as far as his almost ebony eyes.

He proffered a hand as he said, "Hi, I'm Nathan. Can I help you?" His voice was as welcoming as his smile.

I returned his firm handshake and introduced myself.

"Well Craig, what can we do for you?"

"I've been asked to investigate the circumstances behind the death of Rory Kilpatrick, I believe he was a volunteer here."

"That's right, such a tragedy. He was a great help to us."

"Would you mind if I asked you some questions?"

"Not at all, we'll go into the kitchen."

He led me to a door to the left of the stage, it opened onto a corridor that reached behind the stage. The kitchen was at the very back of the building, in what looked like an extension to the original structure.

"Would you like a tea or coffee, Craig?"

" A coffee would be fine, thanks."

He began making the coffee while we chatted.

"So, Craig, why are looking into Rory's death?"

"His mum asked me to have a look as she's not convinced that his death was an accident."

"I did wonder about it myself, the theory seemed a little flawed. But I must admit, I didn't say anything to anyone as I've seen people do some strange things; it comes with the territory."

"Do you mean in here?"

"Well, yes but as I'm a minister, I get to see people at their best and their worst, Craig. A parishioner of mine killed himself, his wife and their two daughters because he had been caught in a fraud at work. Even in Bearsden you get tragedies."

"Are all your volunteers church-goers?"

"No, not all of them, Craig. We have a couple of people from my own church, one or two from parishes nearby but we also have people like Rory with life experience of alcohol and what it can do to them or their loved ones."

He handed me the coffee and sat on a table in the middle of the kitchen while I rested on a cupboard.

"So what do you do here, other than providing food and shelter?"

"If any of our regulars want to try and get sober we will help but we don't preach or cajole, it has to be voluntary. In the main we supply food, a bit of warmth and some company; life can be lonely on the streets."

"Was Rory able to avoid forcing the issue? It must be difficult when drink had devastated his family."

"That's true, Craig, but all of our volunteers understand that you can't force anyone to change their behaviour, they've got to come to a realisation on their own terms, Craig." He seemed to cling to my name like a conversational life raft, repeating it in order to stop him from forgetting it.

"Was there anyone that Rory dealt with regularly, someone he had a connection with?"

"Billy. Billy McInnes, Rory spent some time with him, Craig."

"Is he in tonight?"

"Yes he is, finish your coffee and I'll introduce you."

I drank the coffee and listened to Nathan talk about his ministry. He said that he hoped for an inner city parish but the delicate comfy suburb with coffee mornings and local gossip was what he had been given. He worked at the soup kitchen twice a week, he felt that reaching out to the poor was Christ's calling, not reassuring rich old ladies that they would be going to heaven. I declined to reveal my own thoughts on God and religion.

When we were finished our drinks, Nathan warned me, "Don't give any of the guys any money. That's not why we're here and Billy might chance his arm with you, Craig."

We walked back through to the main hall and I followed Nathan to a group of three figures sitting at one of the gas heaters. They were dressed in a variety of coats in poor repair, a pathetic barrier against the winter's chill. Nathan indicated the man nearest to me, "Craig, this is Billy. Billy, Craig is here to talk about Rory."

"Rory, the boy that died?"

"That's right. Would you like to talk to him, Billy?"

"Aye, don't know whit ah can tell ye, pal, but yir welcome tae ask."

Nathan indicated the door to the kitchen, "Would you like to talk in private?"

"Naw disnae bother me," Billy asserted.

"I'm fine, thanks Nathan."

Nathan took the hint as I retrieved a chair to sit beside Billy. I wished I had placed it a little further back as I was suddenly enveloped in the sour smell of the streets.

Billy was somewhere between 45 and 60 years of age, it was hard to tell as his face was covered in grime, weather beaten into a reddish-brown colour. His eyes were a lifeless grey, a distended red nose occupied the space between them. His hair and beard, peppered with white, were both matted and untidy. He wore a woollen hat on his head, perched insecurely on his tangled mass of hair.

When I was settled, I removed my notebook and pen from inside my leathers. "So Billy how did you and Rory become close?"

He moved around in his seat to face me, "We jist started talkin' wan night, he reminded me a bit of ma boy."

"When was this?"

"Couldnae say for sure but it was a few months before he died."

"What did you talk about?"

"Loadsa stuff, fitba, wimmin, the drink, loadsa stuff."

"What did he say about drinking, did he lecture you?"

"Naw, that wisnae his style. He talked aboot his da, whit happened tae him and how it affected Rory and his ma. He wis honest wi' me and it made me think aboot whit ah hud done. I was even considerin' tryin' tae get sober jist afore he died."

"When did you last see him?"

He paused and he looked away. "It wisnae the Sunday directly afore he wis deid. Must ha' been the week afore that." I wasn't sure if he had been thinking or if he had something to hide.

"How was he that night?"

"No bad, but he wisnae too talkative. Said he hud a lot on at work."

"Did he ever mention anyone he was having problems with?"

Once again he looked away before he said, "Aye, there wis wan guy I remember him sayin' he hud words wi. Somethin' aboot photees of his girlfriend, Isabel or somethin'?"

I nodded to confirm. "Some guy had taken pictures o' her withoot her knowin' aboot it."

"Was his name Derek Norman?"

"Aye that wis him. Rory hud a word wi' him but he told me the guy wis angry wi' him and it nearly came tae blows."

"Is there anything else you remember about Rory in the run up to his death?"

"Naw, that's it."

I felt that he wasn't being entirely honest with me but I decided not to pursue it. "Thanks Billy. If you think of anything else you can tell Nathan to phone me."

"Awright, son. Nae problem."

I put my chair back at the side of the hall before walking towards Nathan. "Was he any help, Craig?"

"Some, but if he remembers anything else I've asked him to tell you to get in touch with me." I handed the cleric my card and we exchanged farewells.

I was glad to get back out into the cold night and took a big breath of the fresh, chilled air.

The visit had been a depressing reminder of how some people struggled to cope with modern life. Alcohol or drugs became an escape before they became a monster, wrapping their tendrils of despair around the unwary victim and dragging them into the depths. I was glad to be on the way to bed and a much needed rest.

Chapter Six

I rose, early on Monday morning, my eyes raw due to lack of sleep. I had already decided to venture to Dolan's place sharp to get his nonsense over. When he was out of my hair, I would take a run to my own office to check if there were any further pieces of insurance work to be dealt with. For the first time I could remember, I was hoping there wouldn't be anything.

The Monday morning traffic was flowing like wallpaper paste and I was once again glad of my nimble form of transport. I passed the frustrated faces of the cramped commuters in their slow moving metal boxes, expressing everything from boredom to the simmering point of road rage. I framed a quiet smile inside my helmet; a bike felt like freedom.

I arrived at Dolan's factory at eight-thirty, the door was already open and the shutters on the windows had been removed. I parked the bike close to the entrance and walked into the factory.

To the left of the door were three offices, old-fashioned wooden partitions with frosted glass, ragged blinds separated the three rooms from the main factory floor and each other. The work of the factory was already underway; a cacophony of different sounds were dominated by the noise of the sewing machines that buzzed like a bee hive disturbed by an apiarist. Beyond the offices seemed to be the area designated for the preparation of the material, the centre was occupied by the sewing machines and the right of the factory was dedicated to finishing and packaging. I guessed there were about 30 people working across the shop floor, the majority of them were women.

The door closest to the entrance opened and Carol stepped out; she was dressed in a navy blue business suit with a simple cream coloured blouse. She beamed a boomerang smile when she realised it was me.

"Mr Campbell, you're early, I thought you were coming in a bit later."

"I thought I might as well get it over with. I think as your accomplice in a robbery you can call me Craig," I answered in a conspiratorial stage whisper.

"Craig it is then. And as your master thief you can call me Carol."

"Is your uncle around?"

"He'll be here in five or ten minutes. Fancy a coffee?"

"Absolutely, have you got any Jamaican Blue Mountain?"

"Funny. It'll be Asda Instant and you'll like it."

"Oh, I'll slum it then."

I followed her into her office and watched as she tinkered

around making the coffee. I sat down in the visitor's chair. The office, a bit like my own, looked a little run down, old furniture on a worn parquet floor with just the slightest hint of a musty smell that was almost masked by the smell of citrus fruit being dispensed by an electronic air freshener.

"Does your uncle know we met?" I wondered out loud.

"No, I thought I would keep it as a nice surprise for him today." She smiled again in an engaging way that stirred something in me.

"This should be fun."

She passed me a brown mug with an insurance company logo decorating it; I sipped the less than fantastic coffee as she settled down in the seat behind her desk.

"So what do you do when you're not working here or prowling the area as a cat burglar?" I asked.

"I like to dance."

"Dance?"

"Yeah, Latin American, like Strictly Come Dancing."

"I see. Not my kind of thing."

"No. You more of a ballet and tap man?" She was in a playful mood.

"Not quite. So do you do this dancing with your boyfriend, then?"

"There's no boyfriend, at the moment." Good news, I thought.

I was about to enquire some more when the office opened and Mr. Dolan walked in.

He looked flustered as he rushed in wearing the same suit he had worn when he visited me. He stopped when he noticed me.

"What the hell are you doing here?" It was good to see that the weekend had helped to refresh his charming persona.

I smiled as pleasantly as I could. "I've come to deliver the report you so kindly paid me for."

"You weren't supposed to be here until this afternoon. I should send you away, Monday mornings are busy enough without you adding to my workload. I suppose you better come into my office." Carol's face cracked into a mischievous smile that she directed at me. Her uncle couldn't see it as he had turned to walk back through the door.

"We'd be as well just talking here, Carol knows why I'm here." He swivelled round, his face wore a fierce scowl, the age lines deepening to canyons.

"She does? How? What have you said?"

"Let's just say I ran into her on Friday night."

"Oh Christ. That's all I need. Don't your lot have client confidentiality?"

"You're thinking of lawyers. I'm sure it's no surprise to you that Carol was your alleged thief. You set this up to teach her a lesson, right?"

"Well, she can't go around stealing from me, after everything I've done for her."

"Uncle John, you know fine well why I'm doing this. It's the only way to make you see sense."

"See sense, see bloody sense? What sense is there in bankrupting me and putting all these folk out there out of work? You know what things are like at the moment." He gesticulated towards the factory floor as he spoke. His anger was beginning to turn his face an even deeper shade of scarlet and I was worried that he might be heading for a heart attack.

In contrast to her Uncle's obvious irritation Carol's voice had a placatory calmness to it, "And what profit would you get from seconds? You know the stores we deal with won't let you sell those fabrics to factory outlets for at least a year. That means they would be sitting in a warehouse costing you money and you wouldn't get half what they cost to make. This way they can do some good for people who don't care what label their clothes have, they're just glad to have them."

I tried to be the peace maker to prevent them saying something they might regret or worse have to call an ambulance for Mr. Dolan. "I've got a suggestion. I'll waive my fee, Mr. Dolan."

At this he brightened and before I could finish he butted in, "Should think so too. I hired you to do a job and you didn't do it right."

"I'll waive my fee on the following conditions. You donate half of it to Carol's charity and you agree to donate some seconds to them every month. You might even get some tax breaks for your charitable work. What do you think?"

Carol was the first to answer, "That sounds fine to me."

Mr. Dolan was silent for some time, the thought that Carol may have got one over him obviously rankled, but eventually he said, "Alright, but no more thieving."

"I won't need to, will I? It's all I wanted to do was put something back." She walked towards him, placed her hand on his arm and gave him a peck on the cheek.

"That's settled then, I better get going and let the two of you sort out the details. Bye Mr. Dolan, no hard feelings?" I stood up and offered Dolan my hand, reluctantly, he shook it but said nothing. I walked to the door and turned to say good-bye to Carol only to find her directly behind me.

"I'll see you out," she said.

When we exited the factory I turned to her. "His bark is a lot worse than his bite isn't it?"

"He's OK really, when you get used to him. Well, I suppose this is good-bye."

I saw my opportunity, "It doesn't need to be. What are you doing on Saturday?"

"Nothing, I think." She smiled and I was relieved that I had read the signals correctly.

"Fancy a run on the bike, away from the Christmas shopping madness?"

"That sounds great, I've done all my shopping anyway."

"You're organised, I've not even started mine. I'll pick you up at 12:30."

"Here's my mobile number." She passed me a business card and then gave me a quick hug before I buttoned up my leathers and put on my helmet. I climbed aboard the Ducati and waved as I headed off into the traffic, an even larger smile now arranged itself on my face.

*

As I still had the details and the key to the storage locker Rory used, I decided to call in on my way to the office. The company was called UR Safe Store and the depot Rory used was in Townhead, just off the M8. It required only a slight diversion from my route and I arrived about 15 minutes after leaving the Dolan's.

It was a large unit, probably a former factory or possibly a warehouse. It was built of a dark brown brick, the colour of aged mahogany, with a grey corrugated roof that looked newer than the majority of the building. Above the simple entrance was a dazzling sign, the company's logo in luminous green and orange, it was probably visible in Edinburgh.

I parked in the customer car park, checked my pockets for the key and the details of the space Rory had rented before I entered the building.

The reception area was painted in a slightly muted version of the logo colours but I thought the staff would need sunglasses to work there all day to avoid splitting headaches. I walked to the desk and pressed a call button as there was no one at the reception. After a short time a man, I guessed was in his early fifties, walked out of an office behind the desk. He was wearing a polo shirt in the now familiar shade of atomic orange with a pair of cheap looking uranium green trousers. He was slight and as angular as a crane, with thinning hair and huge spectacles that made him look like a character from the kids TV channel, Cartoon Network. The badge on his chest told me his name was Robert and that he was the duty manager.

"Yes, sir. How can I help you?" His head bobbed as he spoke as if his jaw was too tight to move on its own.

I decided that I would tell a story approximating the truth.

"I hope you can. A friend of mine rented some space from you a while ago. Unfortunately, he passed away and his girlfriend has asked me to look after his affairs, as you can imagine it's very difficult for her to deal with things at the moment."

He nodded sympathetically, "Do you have the details of the area?"

"I have them here." I handed the paper over to him and he turned to a computer that was sitting on a desk behind the main reception desk. After a few key strokes he looked up, "You're in luck. The bill hasn't been paid for this year's rental and another couple of weeks would have resulted in the locker being opened and the contents auctioned off."

"I'll pay anything that's required for the time that is owed."

"I think, considering the circumstances we can forget about that. Do you have the key as well?"

"I do." I was impressed by his genuine warmth and sympathetic attitude.

"If you'd like to go through the door on the left, I'll meet you on the other side and show you where the locker is."

I followed his instructions and accompanied him through a maze of corridors lined with doors. Judging by the distance between doors there was a large variety of storage sizes available. I guessed that we were close to the back of the building when he finally pointed to a door.

"The lockers are through there, 14c is on the left about half way down. Will you be OK from here?"

"I think I'll manage, thanks."

"Give me a shout if you need anything else."

"Thanks for your help."

I walked through the door into a room lined with pale grey lockers, similar to a swimming pool or sports hall. The light, like most of the building, was a harsh fluorescent yellow that would hurt your eyes if you had to spend any time under it. I walked down the aisle between the lockers and realised that there were more aisles to both the left and right. Beyond a gap that led to the other passageways, I found Rory's compartment. I placed the key in the lock and turned it. Thankfully, it proved to be the correct key and the door swung open.

Inside was a single box that I removed and opened. The box was for an Asus EEE PC netbook computer and the machine was still inside. The ultra-compact computer was taking the tech world by storm and similar machines were now being given away by phone companies desperate for people to sign up for mobile broadband contracts. It looked like it may have already been used, the seal on the packaging was incomplete. I closed the box again and put it into my rucksack. I locked the door and walked back to the reception area. Robert was there waiting for the key, I thanked him for his help and set off for Bridgeton.

*

The short journey to the office was uneventful and I parked the bike ten minutes after leaving the storage company. At the second floor, I nodded to a person waiting to get into the lift whose face was vaguely familiar. I don't know my neighbours in the office building too well but I thought the guy might have something to do with a children's charity that was three doors down from my own.

As I approached my office door it was immediately obvious that something was wrong. It might have been the splinters of wood lying on the floor or the fact the lock was no longer connecting the door to the frame. I'm perceptive that way.

I pushed the door open to a sight of utter chaos; there were papers everywhere, every drawer in the filing cabinet had been forced open and the old PC monitor was smashed into several pieces on the floor. There was no sign of the Mac mini I used as my office PC, the security lock which should have held it to the desk had been cut through with bolt cutters or something similar. The phone was in as many bits as the monitor and the face of the drawers in my desk were broken and lying below the desk. There didn't seem to be a surface or item that hadn't been trashed, torn, wrecked or had disappeared all together.

I backed out the door and used my mobile phone to call the local police station on London Road. I knew it was unlikely that they would find anything incriminating but I wanted to be sure that I didn't touch the contents of the room in case they did decided to dust for fingerprints.

I took off my bike leathers and sat on top of them in the corridor outside the office until the police arrived some forty minutes later.

There were two officers, one male and one female. The female officer introduced them, "Hello Mr. Campbell, I'm Constable Harkness and this is Constable McCulloch."

They were a slightly strange looking couple as she was an inch or two taller than her colleague as well as being broader.

"Can you tell us what happened?"

I gave them a brief account of my absence from the office and what I had discovered upon my arrival.

"What is it you do?" McCulloch asked.

"I'm an independent insurance investigator."

"Do you think this could be related to your work?"

"Possibly, there are plenty people who get annoyed if you come between them and some cash but I've never been threatened."

It was PC Harkness that asked the next question, "Has anything been taken or is it just vandalism?"

"The only thing of any value was my computer, I didn't notice anything else missing, there may be papers but I would have to check."

They went into the office and took some notes but I had the distinct impression that they knew there was little or no chance of finding the culprit. While they worked, I tried to think of anyone who might have been nursing a grudge against me. Although I had caught quite a few people out, the majority were ordinary people, the type who thought they would chance their arm and try to earn a few bob off their insurance company. I couldn't think of anyone that you would call a hardened criminal, someone who would have the character to do something like this.

When the officers were finished they gave me a reference number that I would, ironically, have to pass to my insurance company. I asked about fingerprints but the look I got confirmed that it was way too trivial to waste the resources of the police force on. I thanked them and began the process of clearing up.

I placed the papers on to the desk in roughly alphabetical piles that I would sort in a more thorough manner when there was some semblance of order. I swept up the bits of the monitor and phone using a brush I found in the cleaner's cupboard a couple of doors down from my office. I took particular care with the remains of the monitor as a cathode ray tube was capable of holding a deadly charge.

When that was finished, I looked at the filing cabinet; it was broken beyond repair and I thought I would have to take the documents home with me. There didn't seem much point in sorting them in the office so I put them into a three boxes that the photocopying paper came in. I had no idea how I would get them home on the bike.

I decided that I needed to call the insurance company. I gave the details to a gentleman from the Indian subcontinent and suffered a satellite delay for each response. He agreed that my policy allowed me to call a locksmith to enable me to secure the premises.

I took some photographs of the office with my phone, in case they changed their mind. If anybody knew the vagaries of insurance companies and their policies it was me. The photography complete, I called a directory service that put me through to a local locksmith. I gave him instructions on how to get to the office and he told me he would be there within the hour. By the time he arrived I had tidied up the office to the point that it didn't look like a bomb site.

He was a short man, about 5 feet 4 inches, with a substantial moustache that dominated his face. I reckoned him to be on the retiring side of sixty. His bald pate shone through a drastic comb over that seemed be getting pulled from somewhere below his ear. He wore blue dungarees over a white tee shirt with a pair of substantial safety boots on his feet.

"Aw right, son. Ah'm Boab Williams, the locksmith. You got some damage needing fixed."

"Aye, I need it secured just now," I said as I indicated the door.

"Wee bastards, they should be gi'en a dose o' national service, that would knock the nonsense out their heids," his good natured rant began as soon as he put on his tool bag and continued uninterrupted as he worked at replacing the lock. It was quite entertaining and wandered from the state of the country, "Politicians are the maist useless bunch o' fannies yir ever likely tae meet," through to footballers, "Overpaid prancing nancy boys, they widnae know a day's work if it came and bit them on the arse," finishing with the X-Factor, "Karaoke singers the lot o' them, in fact if you go the Horseshoe Bar ye'll get a better standard o' singer and there's nae Simon Cowell. Although you've goat tae hand it tae the smug prick, he knows how tae make money."

When "Boab" was finished I had a lockable if still damaged door. I paid him the £100 I owed with a cheque and told him that I would call him back when the new door arrived.

"That's nae problem, son. Ah'll look forward tae it. Nice talkin' tae ye." He disappeared in the direction of the lift. Despite what had happened I found myself smiling and I was glad to have met the irrepressible little character.

Now that I had a secure door, I decided to leave the paperwork and maybe borrow Li's Civic the next day to move them to the flat. I left a note for Margaret, the cleaner, explaining what had happened and asking her not to bother with my office tonight. I would give her a key the next time I saw her. By the time all of that was done it was half past four and I thought I would begin the journey home.

*

I went straight home, knowing that Li would be working late. As I was about to turn into Chancellor Street an ambulance pulled out into Byres Road with blue lights flashing and siren blaring. I completed my turn and noticed a police car double parked outside my close. I parked the bike as quickly as I could and rushed over to the entrance to the tenement.

Along the hall was a policeman who was interviewing Mr. Sandison, the man who lived directly opposite Mrs. Capaldi. The policeman looked up at me as I walked towards them, scrutinising me carefully as if I was prime suspect in whatever he was collating information about.

"Excuse me, sir, do you live here?"

"Yes, I'm one floor up."

"Do you know Mrs. Capaldi at all?"

"Yes. Why what's wrong?"

Mr. Sandison answered my question, "Mrs. Capaldi had an accident. They've taken her to the hospital, they think she might have fractured her skull."

In my two years living in Chancellor Street, it was the longest sentence I had ever heard from Mr. Sandison. He was a mouse of a man who seemed to be scared of his own voice or of anyone replying to it.

"Is anyone with her?" I asked, my anxiety made my voice tremble.

"Just the medics, they've taken her over to the Western," the policeman replied.

"Do you know what happened?"

"We're not sure, she fell down a flight of stairs from the first floor landing. Where were you this afternoon, sir?"

"I was dealing with the vandalism of my office in the East End; in fact I was speaking to two of your colleagues. Would it be OK for me to go and see Mrs. Capaldi? I don't want her to be left alone. Has anyone contacted her family?"

"I don't know if we have the details, as yet. Can you help with that?"

"Her son lives out in Dalgety Bay and her daughter's in Norwich. I've got their numbers in my flat upstairs. Do you want to come up?"

"My colleague is up on the first floor landing, pass the details to him while I finish speaking to Mr. Sandison."

I followed his suggestion and walked up to the first floor. The other policeman was older than his mate; he was in his mid to late forties with the signs of middle-aged spread beginning to show. He was inspecting the tread on the stairs, looking closely for anything that may have caused Mrs. Capaldi to fall. I told him my name and what the other officer had asked of me.

"That's fine, sir. Thanks. I'll get it from you in a minute." He continued inspecting the stairwell and the banister.

I had left the outer door of my flat unlocked and when I opened it I saw that the inner door wasn't locked either; the door had been jimmied open.

"Officer," I said with the chills running up and down my spine in athletic spikes.

"Yes, sir."

I indicated the door. He leaned over the banister and called out, "John, you better get up here."

The second policeman climbed the stairs and joined us at the door.

The younger constable was the first one to speak, "You said you were dealing with vandalism at your office, can I ask what it is you do?"

For the second time that day I said, "I'm an independent insurance investigator."

"Looks like you've rattled someone's cage. What are you working on at the moment?"

"I was asked by a mother to look into her son's death. Detective Alex Menzies of 'B' Division knows the details." The younger constable took note of Alex' phone number.

We walked into the flat and it was obvious that the burglar was interrupted in the act. I began to piece together what might have happened.

"I think Mrs. Capaldi must have disturbed whoever was here. She's always kept an eye on this place for me." I felt a deep regret that my gentle, kind and caring neighbour was dragged into this mess.

"Looks that way. We'll get the forensics boys to have a look and see what they can find. Have a quick look round and see if anything is missing but I'm afraid we're going to have to take the place over for a few days as it's now a crime scene."

"Oh. Can I get some clothes into a bag?"

"I wouldn't advise it. I know it's an inconvenience but to give the CID the best chance of catching whoever is responsible, it's better to leave it undisturbed."

I looked around the flat. There wasn't the same level of destruction as there was in the office but it was obvious that someone had been rooting around looking for something. I checked the obvious things but there was no sign of any theft.

"I don't think there has been anything taken unless it was some data from the computer. Is there any chance I can go to see Mrs. Capaldi, I don't want her to be on her own?"

The younger one said, "I'll go with you. We need to be on hand if Mrs. Capaldi wakes up and can remember anything about the attacker. If you can give Constable Jones the details of the family phone numbers we can head over."

I supplied him with the relevant information as well as my mobile number before I picked up my rucksack and helmet.

When I was ready I offered my key, "Here's the key for the outer door of the flat."

"Thanks, we'll be here for a few days, but you should contact your insurance company and get a locksmith out. Here's the incident number," he said passing me a piece of paper from his notebook.

"Thanks."

*

The other policeman told me his name was McInally as we walked towards the hospital. The Western Infirmary, Glasgow's teaching hospital, is a short walk from my flat, so there was no need for a vehicle. From Chancellor Street we crossed Byres Road, walked down to Torness Street and crossed Church Street which brought me to the environs of the hospital. PC McInally led me to the accident and emergency department at the front of the extremely ugly 1960s concrete wart of a building.

We walked to the reception and waited while the nurse finished a phone call.

"Can I help you?" she asked.

"I'm Constable McInally, there was an elderly lady brought in about half an hour ago, a Mrs. Capaldi. We think she may have been attacked and I will need to be nearby when regains consciousness."

"If you take seat, I'll find out what's happening."

"Thank you. This gentleman is Craig Campbell, he's a neighbour of Mrs. Capaldi."

We sat down in the waiting area that contained a variety of people awaiting treatment. On my right was a young boy, about three or four years old, sitting with what I presumed was his mother. His right arm was in a temporary sling and there were tracks of tears on his dirty face. His mother held him in a gentle, protective way; talking to him quietly to reassure him. To my left an elderly man, who looked down on his luck, held a bandage to a cut on his forehead, the bandage was a deep crimson due to the amount of blood it had already soaked up.

The sign warning me to turn off my mobile suddenly caught my attention and I obeyed immediately. I watched the nurse at the reception talk into the phone again for what seemed like an eternity. Eventually she called Constable McNally's name and indicated that we should follow her into a small room.

"Constable, Mrs Capaldi is with the doctors at the moment. She's taken a considerable knock to her head and it looks like her skull is fractured, she also has a broken hip. Constable, if you go to the second floor someone will meet you there." She turned to me, "Are you her next of kin?"

"No, we're neighbours and friends. Her son lives in Fife and her daughter's down south. The police are going to contact them and I imagine Lou, her son, will be here in a couple of hours. I just wanted her to see a familiar face."

"They might be some time with her so you're welcome to wait in here, it's a bit more private."

"Thank you." As I followed her to the waiting room, the policeman headed towards the lift.

When I was settled she walked out the room and left me to my thoughts. I wondered at the sequence of events.

My office had been broken into at some time over the week-end, my flat today. I had no idea what they were looking for but it was obvious I had caught the attention of somebody. I wondered if the netbook held the key.

I lifted the box out of my bag. I removed the computer from the box and switched it on. It booted into the Ubuntu Linux operating system and unlike Rory's home PC, it was password protected. I knew my way around computers, not enough to hack a password but I knew a man who would, Barry. I added a visit to Barry to my mental to do list. I put the laptop back into the box and then into the bag.

I felt hungry and remembered noticing a vending machine on my way in to the hospital. I walked to it and bought some crisps, a bar of chocolate and a can of Coke. In the room I ate without any real sense of taste, it was just calories to keep me going.

After nearly an hour the nurse came back into the room. "Mr Campbell, if you would like to come with me."

I followed her out to the lifts and she told me to go to the second floor where I was to ask for a nurse called Laura Bryant in the intensive care unit.

The lift deposited me on the second floor and I followed the signs to the ICU. I washed my hands with the disinfect-ant hand wash from a dispenser that are present across the NHS, a weapon in the attempt to combat the superbugs that are plaguing British hospitals.

I pressed the intercom and awaited a reply.

"Yes?"

"Hi, I'm here to see Mrs. Capaldi. I was told to ask for Laura Bryant."

"One moment, please."

After a short pause the door swung open and a young nurse in blue scrubs appeared, "Hi, I'm Laura."

Once again I was ushered into a family waiting room.

"Mr. Campbell, are you a relative?"

"No, but I'm the closest thing she has at the moment until her son arrives."

"Well I'm afraid she's very ill. She has what is called a Linear Fracture to the back of her skull. The doctors have sent her for a CT scan which confirmed what the paramedic thought at the scene. She is in a coma at the moment. We are monitoring her very closely as we are concerned about a build-up of pressure from internal bleeding within the skull. Her heart is very weak and we will only operate on her if the pressure becomes life threatening but it is very high risk. Ideally, we would move her to the Southern General, where the leading neurology specialists are but that is also too risky at the moment. I'm afraid she may not survive no matter what we do."

My heart dropped through my stomach and I felt the tears well in my eyes. I nodded at the nurse in a numb daze.

"We're keeping her comfortable at the moment and she is more stable now than when we she came in."

"Can I see her?" my voice crackled with emotion as I spoke.

"If you give us about ten minutes you can come in. Can I get you anything, a cup of tea or coffee?"

"A cup of coffee, please."

The nurse went to make the coffee and left me alone. I could hear the faint sound of machines beeping from the rooms within the ward. The air was humid and the room felt claustrophobic. I stood up and walked the short distance to the window but the view was the back of another building within the hospital complex. I thought about Mrs. Capaldi's family and how this would devastate them. Despite the distance between them and their mother they were a close family; they both called her often and visited her when they could.

Nurse Bryant returned and I drank the coffee as something to do while I waited, it provided neither nourishment nor pleasure. Ten minutes soon became twenty, which quickly ticked over to thirty.

I was beginning to feel myself drifting off to sleep because of the heat in the room when the door opened and the nurse said, "Mr. Campbell you can come in now. I have to warn you that she has lots of tubes in her and we have immobilised her head and neck, so she looks a lot different from what you are used to."

She lead me past the nurses station, to a room three doors away on the left side of the corridor. I was aware how busy the ward was with staff everywhere, as you would expect in an ICU.

When I walked into the room the shock almost took my breath from me. Despite the warning the nurse had given me it was still disturbing to see the dramatic change from the zestful lady I knew so well. She now looked like a shell of a human being, lying still in a bed. She seemed to have visibly diminished, her skin was a rain cloud grey colour, her head was shaved in preparation for any surgery that might be required. There were machines monitoring her condition and some administering drugs automatically to help her body deal with the trauma. Constable McNally was sitting in a visitor's chair to the left of the bed. His hat was on his lap and he nodded toward me as I entered. I swallowed a sob and remembered reading about the importance of positive energy for coma victims.

I stepped towards the bed and held her hand, her skin was paper dry and almost translucent. It was pierced by a cannula to allow the medical staff to draw blood. "Hi Mrs C. it's your favourite neighbour. What are you doing lying in that bed, I thought you were going to take me dancing?" I prattled on in a similar fashion for a while, conversing with her as if she was answering me in her usual cheeky way.

The nurse asked me to leave the room after about fifteen minutes and I went back to the waiting area. Around eight, the door opened and Lou Capaldi walked in. I hugged him as the tears poured down both of our faces. He was in his late forties, his handsome Latin features slipping gently towards middle-age.

"Oh Craig, do you know what happened?" he asked when he could find his voice.

"It looks like your mum disturbed someone that was breaking into my flat and they knocked her down the stairs. I'm so sorry, Lou."

"You don't have to apologise, you didn't do it. I know what Mum is like, she's always looking out for folk."

"Thank you, but I feel so responsible and you know how well we get on with each other, she's like a second mum to me. Have you spoken to a doctor or a nurse?"

"Yes, I spoke to a Doctor Patel and she let me know how ill Mum is. They'll send someone through when I can go in to see her."

"Do you know the police are with her?"

"Yes, the doctor said."

"Did someone get a hold of Maria?"

"Yes, I phoned her. She'll be up on the first flight she can get from London."

The conversation drifted into silence as we waited, Lou's occasional sob was the only thing to break the silence. We sat for another twenty minutes before Laura, the nurse came in again.

"Mr. Capaldi, do you want to come in now?"

Lou stood up, "Can you come in with me, Craig?"

"Are you sure?"

"Aye, I could do with someone to support me."

As we walked along the corridor, Laura gave the same speech to Lou she had given me about being prepared but I knew it would be inadequate. Lou's audible gasp on seeing his mother almost started me off again. He cried loudly for several minutes before he could compose himself and go to her bedside. I stood behind him, feeling his pain batter against me like a violent sea storm. We remained in that little diorama of grief for some fifteen minutes.

I noticed the monitor beside the bed as Mrs. Capaldi's heart rate and blood pressure began to rise. The alarms started to sound insistently and Laura, another nurse and two doctors rushed in.

"Can you all leave, please?" one of the doctors framed it as a question but her tone indicated that it was really an order.

"What's happening? Please tell me what's happening." Lou shouted his question.

Doctor Patel replied, "Mr Capaldi, we need you to leave to allow us to help you mother, her body is reacting to the trauma, we'll come and tell you when she's stable again."

Constable McInally used a sympathetic, gentle force to move Lou out of the room. We had walked only a short distance when Lou fell to the floor, the stress and grief combined to remove the power from his legs. I took one arm, while the constable took the other and we helped him back to the waiting room. I went to the cooler that occupied a space in the corner of the room and poured a cup of chilled water for Lou.

"Thank you. Oh Craig, I hope she's going to be OK. What am I going to do?"

"I don't know Lou. The doctors will do all they can."

I held him in a gentle hug while he cried more quietly. The minutes seemed to drag as we waited on the doctors.

It was around ten when Doctor Patel walked into the room and it was obvious from the look on her face that it wasn't good news.

"Oh no. Oh no. Oh my god no." Lou read her look the same way that I had. I stood up and allowed her to sit beside him and take his hands in hers.

"Mr. Capaldi I'm very sorry but I'm afraid there's nothing we can do. Your mother sustained a very serious fracture to the back of her skull and internal bleeding has led to pressure on her brain that has led to a shut down of the core functions of her body. We are keeping her alive using a ventilator but I'm afraid she will never come out of the coma."

Lou kept up a mantra of "Oh no" as he absorbed the doctor's words.

"If you wish we can keep her on the ventilator until your sister gets here and that would give you both a chance to say good-bye."

Lou managed a nod but couldn't say anything. The grief now enveloped him and he cried as hard as any man I had ever seen. I stood with tears tumbling down my face, weeping for him and for the friend I had lost.

McInally left the room, I presumed that he would be going to tell his fellow officers that they were now dealing with a murder investigation. He was replaced by Laura Bryant, the nurse who came in to console us.

She stayed with us after the doctor left, she expressed her sympathies and offered to get tea or coffee. We both refused and sat in silent contemplation of a future without that gentle soul who had so enriched our lives.

I waited with Lou until Maria arrived. I left the two of them to spend some time together and walked to Mrs. Capaldi's room. Laura was there, adjusting machines and tending to her patient; she smiled a sad smile as I walked in.

Once again I held Mrs. Capaldi's hand and spoke quietly into her ear, "I'll get whoever did this to you, I promise. I'm going to miss you, Mrs C. You are a wonderful lady and you don't deserve this." I kissed her forehead, "Good-bye, sweet lady." A slow tear trickled down my face and landed on her lips, I kissed it away, laid her hand back on the bed and walked out of the room.

On leaving the hospital I called Li , told him what had happened and that I was going to be out of my flat for a few days. He offered me a bed on his living room floor that I was relieved to accept.

Li opened the door of his flat in Byres Road with a look of both shock at what had happened and concern for me.

"How you doin', man?"

"I've been better. Thanks for this."

"No problem. Have you had anything to eat?"

"I'm OK mate, I don't feel very hungry, although I could do with a decent cup of coffee if you've got one."

As he fussed around me and organised coffee, I called my mother.

"Hi Mum."

"What's wrong?"

"Mrs. Capaldi's dead."

"Oh no Craig, what happened?"

The words stuck in my throat as the grief overtook me again and I passed the phone to Li.

"Hello Mrs. Campbell, it's Li." I listened to one side of the conversation.

"He's a bit shaken up."

"It looks like Mrs. Capaldi disturbed a burglar in Craig's flat and that they pushed her down the stairs in the close."

"Nobody seems to know."

After listening for a short time Li turned to me, " Your mum's wondering if she can do anything to help."

I shook my head, "I'll ring her tomorrow, tell her. Oh and tell her I love her."

"He's OK just now but he'll ring you tomorrow. I've to tell you he loves you."

"I will Mrs. Campbell. Bye." He returned the phone."She loves you too and I've to look after you."

After I drank the coffee, the rigours of the day overtook me and I felt devoid of energy. Li was quick to become aware of my exhaustion and started to put a bed together for me on the living room floor. When it was ready he said, "Looks like you need a kip. I'll get to bed and I'll see you in the morning. I'm really sorry about Mrs. Capaldi, Craig. I know how much she meant to you."

"Thanks mate. Good night."

I settled down to sleep but despite my exhaustion, I couldn't get my brain to rest. I tossed and turned, listening as the pubs emptied and the raucous customers dissipated into the night. The road outside the window became quiet with only an occasional engine to disturb the tranquillity. It was the only time of day that Byres Road wasn't packed with traffic, either pedestrian or vehicular. I stared at the ceiling and slowly a steely resolve began to form itself. The people behind Rory's death were also guilty of at least two other deaths. I was convinced that there was more than one person involved and that would indicate money, probably a significant sum. I needed to understand why Rory died, only then would I be able to trace Mrs. Capaldi's killer and there was nothing I wanted more than to catch him or her. Now I wasn't only hunting the faceless killer of a man I didn't know, now I needed to catch them and see them punished for Lou, Maria but most of all for Mrs. Capaldi.

Chapter Seven

Eventually sleep did come but by quarter to seven I was wide awake again. Li came through fifteen minutes later.

"How you doing? Did you sleep?"

"A little."

"I'm going to get ready for work. Go and have a rake through my wardrobe, see if there's anything there you fancy. Don't want you smelling the place out." There was little humour in his smile.

"Thanks, Li. Are you using the car today?"

"No, I'll take the underground. Do you need it?"

"I've got to collect some stuff from my office." In my despair of the previous night, I had forgotten to tell him about the break in at the office or the netbook computer I found in the storage centre. I gave him a quick summary of the events of the previous day.

"This is serious, Craig. Surely the police have got to sit up and take notice. They must do something."

"To be honest, I don't give a shit what they think or do. I'm going to get the bastard behind this." He looked shocked at the vehemence of my statement.

"Craig, this is a real evil bastard and he's not going to let you get in his way."

"We'll see about that," I said as the anger began to burn.

"Just be careful, man."

"Thanks for your concern Li, but I'll be ready."

Li finished his preparations for work and left me the keys to the Civic before he set off.

I roused myself from my makeshift bed and had a quick shower. After looking through Li's clothes I picked out a tee shirt, a pair of boxers and socks.

Washed and dressed, I had another coffee but again the thought of food was not in the least bit appealing. I sat with the coffee, called my mother to reassure her that I was fine and that she didn't need to come running to my rescue. She lived in Arbroath, in a little retirement flat close to the sea shore and I didn't want her having to make a long trip to Glasgow in the depths of a Scottish winter. After several reassurances she finally gave in and I told her I would see her at Christmas.

I called David Stone next. "Hi, it's Craig Campbell."

"Oh hi, Craig."

"Sorry to disturb you but I was wondering if there's any chance we can meet again?"

"Today?"

"Yes, if possible. I've got some questions about Derek Norman. Do you think you could get some information for me from the girls in the office that have had problems with him?"

"I'll try, but I don't know if they'll speak to me. I'll do what I can."

"Oh and can you dig out the details for Rory's boss for me?"

"Joe Callaghan, will do."

"I'll get you in the Counting House at George Square about 5?"

"OK, I'll see you then"

He hung up and I dialled Alex' number.

"Hi Craig, how are you getting on?"

I told her about the previous day and night. I also filled her in on the death of Brian Swanson.

"I'll check that one out but you need to turn this over to us now, Craig."

"Do you think that they'll act now?"

"I certainly hope so. Do you want me to speak to the BT Police?"

"If you think it'll do any good. But I've got to warn you Alex, I'm still going to follow this to the bitter end."

"You get in the way and it's you that'll end up in jail." Her tone was that of an officer of the law rather than an anxious friend.

"I don't care, as long as I've put the murderer there first. Have a look at that other accident for me, please."

"Craig, for Christ's sake did you not hear what I said?"

"Look, get the information and I'll look after myself."

"Fine, but this is the last. I'm not helping you get yourself arrested or maybe worse." The call ended abruptly.

My mobile rang immediately.

"Hello."

"Mr. Campbell?"

"Yes."

"Hello Mr. Campbell, it's Constable Jones. We need you to come into the station for fingerprinting and we'll need a statement from you."

"Oh, yes. No problem, when do you want me?"

"If you could come in about eleven this morning that would be fine."

I checked my watch, it was half nine. "OK."

"Do you know where we are?"

"Dumbarton Road isn't it?"

"That's right, beyond the railway station on the left. We'll see you then."

*

I sat for an hour watching some daytime television show on antiques, not really paying attention, the voices a distant drone. I locked up Li's flat and walked down to Chancellor Street to retrieve my bike. I noticed the crime scene tape at the bottom of the stair in my close. The police had said that the communal area should be clear within a day but that the flat would be investigated by the scene of crime officers for a couple of extra days.

On the way to the police station, I stopped at a news-agent to buy a paper. Mrs. Capaldi's death was reported on the fifth page. It gave a brief account of the break in, a photograph of the police outside the tenement close and a little about Mrs. Capaldi. There was a quote from Mr.

Sandison, blaming neds for the death of his "lovely neigh-bour". I thought it was ironic, as my neighbour thought he was a bit peculiar because he didn't talk to anyone, least of all her.

I completed the short ride and parked the bike in the small car park to the left of the police station. I walked through the entrance of the modern brick building and up to the reception desk. I introduced myself to the officer behind the desk and he called through to PC Jones.

"Come through, Craig. This shouldn't take too long," Constable Jones said when he appeared. He escorted me to a desk in a crowded office where he placed my hands on a scanner. The machine worked away capturing an impression of my unique loops, arches and whorls.

When he was finished he said, "DC Cooper will take your statement regarding Mrs. Capaldi's death. If you would please follow me. I'm sorry we're a little short of space at the moment, so I'm afraid it's an interview room."

"That's OK,' I said feeling far from comfortable.

As instructed, I followed him to the interview room, decorated in bureaucratic beige, furnished with the mini-malism that a Scandinavian designer could only dream of; a single table with chairs for four people and a tape recorder. I sat in a chair on the side furthest from the door as I believed that would be the form for such chats.

Detective Cooper arrived shortly after I had settled, she sat beside Jones on the opposite side of the table from me. She was in her early thirties, tall and broad for a woman. She wore her coal black hair pulled back from her face in a way that made her look like someone after a severe face lift. Some of the skin on the right of her face was scarred white by a burn. In contrast the rest of her complexion was a ruddy, weather beaten brown. I guessed that she maybe spent some time climbing or hill-walking.

"I hope this room is alright, Mr. Campbell, I know it's not ideal but it is the best place to allow us to talk in private." Her accent had a trace of Ayrshire, her voice a lower register than some men I knew. She was not a lady I would like to have crossed in any way.

"It's fine thanks."

She began by asking me about my relationship with Mrs. Capaldi. I told her about our jokes, how I shopped for her occasionally and how she looked out for me. I found it difficult to talk about her in the past tense and the officers were sympathetic in the pacing of their questions.

"Now can we move on to the break-ins," Cooper said. "The investigation you are conducting, can you give me some detail?"

I told her about Mrs Kilpatrick's visit, my subsequent suspicions based on what I had discovered of Rory's character and the fact that I asked Alex to have a look at the BT Police reports.

"Is there anything that might have provoked the break-ins, documents or photographs, anything that the culprit might believe implicated anyone?"

I decided not to tell them about the key, the storage locker or the netbook computer. "So far I haven't found anything that would amount to evidence, everything I've got is based on the stories I have heard from people and their impressions of Rory as a person. Maybe whoever it was broke in thinking I had something incriminating , but I've got nothing that you would call proof."

"It looks like you've spooked someone. Are you planning to document your thoughts and hand them to the BTP?"

"Would you accept a case based on what I've told you?"

"Probably not but Mrs. Capaldi's death puts a new spin on it. We'll have to liaise with them and hopefully they'll be willing to co-operate but I know they are even more stretched for resources than we are. It might be that we can persuade them to let us run with it, as part of the same investigation."

"I hope so, Rory's mother is looking for justice and with the best will in the world there is only so much I can do."

"We would prefer that you don't do anything else, Mr. Campbell, in connection with this investigation and you definitely don't want to get in our way as far as Mrs. Capaldi's death goes."

Her tone rankled me, "I'll not be in anyone's way. If you get the BTP to play ball then I'm out, if not I'm going to pursue this until I've got something substantial that you can use."

"I really don't think that's wise."

"Well that's the way it's going to be." I replied with more anger than was sensible when talking to a police detective, particularly one who looked like she could crush me like an old cola can.

"We'll speak to BTP, please don't do anything until after that discussion." She was offering me a small olive branch and although I had no intention of walking away I said, "OK."

She changed tack, "Is there anyone else who might have it in for you?"

"There might be some people I've pissed off over insurance claims but I doubt it would be enough for them to break into my home as well as my office."

"Would you mind giving us some names of people that you have "pissed off" as you put it?"

I gave her three names of dodgy characters that were upset at me for proving their claims to be as authentic as a Van Gogh still-life that included a mobile phone; I believed it to be a waste of time but I wanted to show willing as I had probably annoyed her enough that day.

She gave me her card and I reciprocated. The interview over, I shook hands and said my farewells. Officer Jones escorted me back to the main door.

"It might be better if you do as she says you know."

I gave a noncommittal nod, turned and walked away without a reply.

*

I spent the afternoon in Li's flat, dozing on the couch as I tried to catch up on my lost sleep. My dreams were haunted by Mrs. Capaldi, looking so devoid of life on the hospital bed. She suddenly opened her eyes and looked up at me as if pleading with me to help her.

The nightmare disturbed me into wakefulness, tears streamed down my face. When I had calmed down, I showered to help give me some energy.

At around four, I set out to meet Stone and try to find out more about Derek Norman.

I parked the bike in a space on West George Street and strolled the short distance back to George Square and the Counting House pub.

The pub was in a huge space once occupied by a branch of the Bank Of Scotland. Completed in 1870, the building design was influenced by the Italian renaissance and has an ornate ceiling topped with a glass dome. The walls are decorated in the warm pastels of Tuscany rather than the gelid grey of the West of Scotland and are adorned with reminders of the building's previous occupants. The floor space is vast but it's always been difficult to find a table, in what has been one of Glasgow's favourite watering holes since it opened in 1996.

I was a little early for the meeting, so I ordered a fresh orange and stayed close to the door while I waited for David Stone to arrive.

I had time to look around at the animated faces of the customers as they struggled to make themselves heard above the noise of everyone else trying to make themselves heard. There was no music in the pub but there always seemed to be a cacophony of conversation as the voices of the patrons were magnified by the echo of the cathedral-like dimensions of the room. Business suits were the most common mode of dress for both the men and women. A lot of people had escaped the office and stopped for a pint on the way home. I thought of how Rory's father escaped the pressures of his job by diving into a bottle and wondered how many around me would end up taking the same route.

My thoughts were interrupted when Davie Stone walked in. He was also dressed in a suit, a dark blue pin-stripe but it looked like a cheap purchase from his local supermarket. The material looked frayed in places and faded in others. The knot in his tie was loose and the top button of his sky blue shirt was undone. He spotted me and came to join me.

"Hi Davie, what you for?" I asked.

"A pint of IPA, please."

I caught the attention of a barman, ordered the pint and another orange juice for myself. When we had been served, we looked around for a table. We found a two seater tucked away in a corner, overlooking George Square.

When Stone had wrestled out of his suit jacket and we were settled into our seats I began my questions, "Any luck with the girls?"

"A couple of them and one more that would like to talk to you personally."

"OK. What did you find out?"

"Derek Norman's a creep and that he should be locked up. The two girls I spoke to who were willing to talk don't want me to tell you their names, I think they're genuinely scared of the guy."

"That's OK, I don't need their details, I just need to build up a better picture of him."

He leaned towards me from the opposite side of the table, his voice reduced to conspiratorial level, "He arrived in our office about four years ago. He'd been doing some similar work in Newcastle but upped sticks and moved to Scotland. We've heard rumours that he had to leave Newcastle in a hurry but I don't know how true they are."

He took a deep draught of his pint before continuing. "The first girl I spoke to had problems with him not long after he arrived. She had tried to be nice to him, just trying to be friendly to the new guy kind of thing. He seemed to get the wrong end of the stick and he asked her out. She said that she was polite in turning him down but he went mental at her. He said that she was like all the others, a tease who would lead a guy on, only to let him down. He was screaming at her and then stormed off."

"Was this in the office?"

"No, he asked her as she was walking to catch her bus after work one Friday. This was about three weeks after he arrived in our place. He apologised to her on the Monday but she was really unnerved by it. She waits for one of the other girls before she'll leave the office to go home."

"Sounds like our man's got quite a temper. He was less than calm when he threw me out of his flat. What about the other girl you mentioned? Did she have a similar experience?"

Stone became animated as he said,"No, she had the really creepy one. She came to work with us about four months after Norman arrived. She's an accountant and has to work with Norman from time to time. He would ask her where she lived, what bus she got home, where she shopped. At first she thought he was just taking an interest in her to be polite but as time went on she began to get a bit freaked out by it.

You should see him when he's talking to women, it's almost as if he's a big cat checking out the prey. It's no wonder the girls are scared of him, there's something disturbing about him. Anyway, one Saturday this woman comes out of her local supermarket and there's the bold Norman standing outside. She lives in Williamwood on the south side. She approached him to try and warn him off but he said he was there to get a gift for a friend that he was going to visit."

"Did she make a formal complaint to the police or anyone in your office?"

He shook his head. "No, I asked her that. She didn't want to make a fuss, she just wanted to forget about it."

"Were both of these women single at the time that this happened?"

"Yes. Although I think the second girl is going out with someone now."

"Did any of them know any more about the incident with the phone?"

"No, but one of the guys remembered a bit more about it. Rory was in a meeting with this guy Thomas Granger, Norman and one or two others. The meeting was over and Norman had left his phone on the table. Rory picked it up and accidentally pressed a button that lit up the screen. Norman had a picture of Isabel as his wallpaper. Rory told Granger that Isabel obviously didn't know it was being taken. Rory shut the meeting room door and had it out with Norman. Norman was fuming when he came out and took the afternoon off, claiming he was feeling ill."

"How long before Rory's death did this happen?"

"A few weeks I think."

"That's great Davie, it's good information." I responded with enthusiasm.

"You're welcome, anything to help."

"What about the other woman that wants to speak to me?"

"Audrey, Audrey Bruce. She's a character, Audrey, I think she'll have plenty to say but how much is relevant is another thing. She's nice enough but she does like the sound of her own voice." He grinned at a private joke that he didn't share with me.

"Did you get that phone number for me?"

"Yes, I'll send it to your phone." He retrieved his mobile phone from his inside jacket and pressed some buttons before my own phone acknowledged receipt of the details with a simple bell.

"Thanks for that."

"I'll need to go, I don't like to leave my mother too long."

"Does someone look after her while you're at work?"

"There's a home help comes in to give her some lunch but other than that it's just me."

"Must be tough on you, looking after her on your own all the time."

"What can you do? She did it for me when I was young, so now it's my turn."

"Tell her I was asking for her. Thanks again."

"See you." He gulped the last of his pint of beer, shook my hand and disappeared into the crowd. I finished my orange juice before setting out for home.

*

When I was back in the flat, I found Callaghan's number on my mobile and pressed the green button to initiate the call.

After three rings a woman's voice answered, "Hello, Eileen Callaghan speaking."

"Hello. Can I speak to Mr. Callaghan please?"

"I'm sorry he can't come to the phone. Can I take a message?"

"My name is Craig Campbell, is there any chance I could make an appointment to come and speak to him?"

"What do you want to speak to him about?"

"A former colleague of his, Rory Kilpatrick."

"That's the lad that was killed in that terrible accident, isn't it?"

"Yes. I'm trying to get some information on what happened leading up to Rory's death, I believe Mr. Callaghan was Rory's boss for a while."

"That's right. I don't know how much help he'll be but I suppose it would be OK."

"Would tomorrow evening be convenient, say about four o'clock?"

"OK."

She gave me an address in Wemyss Bay on the Clyde Coast. I wondered if she'd been his secretary before she was his wife; she showed the same kind of reluctance to let me speak to him as I would get from a PA at an insurance company.

Li called at around six-thirty and said he would bring some pizza in. As I was in no mood to cook I agreed wholeheartedly to a chicken and mushroom, stone-baked from the local take-away.

He arrived home at seven and we ate exchanging stories of our day like a married couple. For the rest of the night we vegetated on the sofa watching catch up episodes of Lost and Heroes.

Chapter Eight

The following morning I was up and about before Li. I decided to repay his kindness by making him breakfast. I found some eggs in the back of the fridge that were still within their sell-by date. I scrambled them, poured some cereal into a bowl and placed a glass of orange juice on the table as Li walked in.

"Thanks, man, this is brilliant. I never eat this well in the mornings."

I brewed a coffee for us and left him to finish his breakfast while I sat on the couch, reading the paper I had bought the previous day.

When Li was finished, he left for work.

I felt a bit stiff and sore from sleeping on the floor, so I put myself through a half hour programme of stretches and exercise to loosen my limbs, get my blood flowing and work off some of the calories from the pizza. I felt better for my work out particularly after a bracing shower. I raided Li's wardrobe again and was ready to face the challenges of the day ahead.

I decided to give Audrey Bruce a call, the woman that was so keen to speak to me. It was the second time her name had come up as she was also on the list of colleagues that Mrs. Kilpatrick had given me. She was another member of the PPP section that Rory had worked in. The number Mrs. Kilpatrick gave me was an office number and I dialled it.

The phone was answered by an effeminate male voice, "Good morning, City Council, Simon speaking."

"Good morning, can I speak to Audrey Bruce, please?"

"Certainly, may I say who is calling?"

"My name is Craig Campbell."

"One moment, please." The sound of muzak filled my ears for a few seconds before I was connected.

"Hello, Audrey Bruce speaking."

"Hi Audrey, I was wondering if it would be possible to speak to you about Rory Kilpatrick?"

"I'm sorry I won't be able to deal with your request over the phone. If you send an e-mail I might be able to help you." Her voice sounded strained and false, I found it puzzling as she was keen to speak to me according to Stone.

"OK. Can you give me your e-mail address?"

She supplied the information and ended the call abruptly.

I used Li's computer to send mail from my web mail service. I detailed what I was trying to do and how I hoped she would be able to help me.

While I awaited a reply, I made another cup of Li's strong espresso coffee to pass the time as much as anything else. I read through the backlog of e-mails I had, one from an insurance company checking some details of a case I had completed for them a month previously. I would need to go to the office to try and dig out the documents from the mess that was my filing system.

The reply from Audrey arrived about half an hour after I sent the original.

Mr. Campbell,

I'm sorry about earlier but after everything that has happened in here I am trying to be careful. Derek Norman was just outside the office.

I can meet you at the corner of Buchanan Street and St. Vincent Street at 12:00 tomorrow. Stand beside the Orange phone shop.

Audrey Bruce

She was obviously cautious of something. Maybe it was Derek Norman but it all seemed a bit melodramatic. I wondered if she was enjoying a joke at my expense or whether she was a little paranoid. I typed a reply agreeing to her request and sent it back, hoping that I wasn't wasting my time.

*

With some time on my hands before I had to meet Callaghan I decided to put it to good use. My discussion with Billy in the soup kitchen had been nagging away at the back of my mind since Sunday night. The feeling that he was holding something back was persistent and I didn't want to wait until the following Sunday to discover what it was.

I suited up in my leathers, climbed on the bike, and set off to look for an anonymous itinerant man in a city that didn't know or care that he existed.

I started with a trip to the soup kitchen building but it was closed to mercy, the homeless left to fend for themselves during the day. I had no idea where the under-class of the city would go during daylight hours. There were other shelters, some offering a bed and I tried a number of them but they had either never heard of Billy or hadn't seen him in a while. The last place I tried was in the east end of the city and one of the volunteers said he thought that Billy went to an abandoned factory in Polmadie on winter days. I thanked him and rode the short distance to the address he had given me.

The factory looked like an old engineering works, a remnant of Glasgow's industrial past. It dated from the 1930's and was built of crumbling dark red brick, ruptures ran through the mortar as if it had survived the tremors of an earthquake. The windows were all broken, the ground surrounding it cracked and strewn with rubble. The enormous steel door had been turned a vibrant red by oxidation; a sign on it prohibited entry, stating unequivocally that the building was dangerous.

After parking the bike on the only piece of level tarmac I could find, I walked to the human-sized entrance that was cut into the main door. It was slightly ajar and groaned a loud complaint when I pushed it further, oxidised metal scraped on oxidised metal, the sound of a wounded dinosaur. Inside the there was a vast single space, lit dimly from the shattered windows and the gaps in the corrugated iron roof. Below the roof line, an overhead crane sat in desolate silence, rust spread across it like a fungus. At the centre of the structure, an oil barrel acted as a radiator; burning wood created flames that moved with a crackling dance, lighting the faces of the bodies gathered around it.

They turned in unison at the noise from the door, regarding me with suspicion. One or two moved to a position of safety behind the drum, others took a more aggressive posture as they stepped towards me. As I approached, I counted about fifteen men ranging in age from early twenties to sixty, some of them defied classification, life on the streets giving them an ageless mien.

A younger man with a heavy beard stepped forward, "Whit the fuck dae ye want? Ur ye loast?" An Alpha male in a pack of Omegas.

"I'm not here to cause you any trouble, I'm looking for Billy McInnes. I was told that he came here occasionally."

"Whit dae ye want him fur?"

"I need to speak to him about something we talked about earlier in the week, at the soup kitchen."

"Mebbe he disnae want tae talk tae you?"

"Look if he's not here, I'll leave you in peace."

"Shug, it's aw right, ah know this guy." Billy stepped from behind the oil drum, he looked smaller than I remembered; he clutched a cheap bottle of tonic wine in his right hand and looked unsteady on his feet.

"Ur ye sure, ah'll boot him oot if ye want?" Shug was not ready to back down.

"Naw, s'awright. Craig, how ye doin', man? Whit brings ye tae the social event o' the decade?" He gestured extravagantly, indicating his fellows and the surroundings. He lead me away from the group towards a deteriorating wall.

"Billy, I need to talk to you. I don't think you told me everything on Sunday and I was hoping that you might be able to open up without Nathan hanging around."

"There's nuthin' else tae say, know. Ah've toald ye everythin' ah kin." His words were slurred and his eyes were touched by an alcoholic glaze.

"When I asked when was the last time you saw Rory, you hesitated, as if you were wondering whether to tell me the truth. I'm not sure you decided that the truth was the way to go."

"Look, man, yir awright but ah jist want tae keep ma heid doon. Ah kin find enough trouble masel' withoot your help."

"Billy, I don't need to tell anyone where I got the information. I'm not a cop, I'm just a man trying to help a woman that lost her son. Rory's mother deserves to know how Rory died, to give her some peace."

"Ah know, he wis a good guy." He hung his head, almost physically contemplating his naval. He appeared to come to a decision.

"Ah saw him the night he died."

I was surprised and my voice rose an octave when I asked,"Where?"

"Doon in a lane aff Argyle Street, cannae remember the name o' it."

"When was this?"

"It wis late, ah wis jist dossin' doon for the night in a doorway. Rory went past wi' two big guys, looked like bouncers. They never noticed me. Wan guy hud a strong grip on Rory's erm and he was tellin' him tae be quiet or somethin' bad wid happen tae Rory's girlfriend. They walked doon tae the darkest bit o' the alley and the next thing ah know wan o' the big guys gies Rory a dillion in the guts. Rory doubled up and the guy started layin' intae him wi' his boot and his fists. Ah wis shittin' masel' so ah wis, jist lay there as still as ah could. When he finished, he goat a phone oot and spoke tae somebody. Couple minutes later a moator appeared, the big guy and the driver bundled him intae the back seat and the moator drove aff. The two big guys walked away doon the lane towards the river."

"Did you see the big guys' faces?"

"Naw it wis too dark and when they started tae beat the shit oot 'im, ah jist stoapped watchin'"

"Why didn't you tell anyone?"

"Like who, the polis. They bastards wid have told me tae piss aff back tae ma jakey hole."

"Can you remember anything else?"

"Ah think wan o' them wis English but ah'm no sure. He talked funny. It wis a while a go and ma memory's no whit it wis. The bevvy'll dae that tae ye."

"Billy you've been a big help." I reached into my pocket and offered him a ten pound note. He looked reluctant at first but then reached for it.

"Ta."

"Try to get yourself something decent to eat. If you remember anything else get Nathan to phone me."

"Aye nae worries. Ah hope ye get the bastards."

I left him to walk back to his little cadre. I doubted that my ten pounds would buy him much more than a sandwich and a large bottle of something destructive. I knew that there was nothing I could do to help him, he had to help himself.

I had to concentrate on what I needed to do about the information Billy had given me. His description of at least one of the culprits, as far as it went, fitted Derek Norman. Whether it was him was still something I needed to prove.

*

It was time to visit Mr. Callaghan. I climbed aboard the bike and set off for the Firth of Clyde. The journey down the M8, onto the A78 was uneventful and I arrived in Wemyss Bay at three o'clock, an hour too early. I decided to have a quick coffee in Largs, another ten minutes further down the coastal road.

Largs is for many people in the West of Scotland, a place of nostalgia. Nardini's tea room was famous throughout the country for some of the best ice cream you ever tasted and rose-tinted, hindsight spectacles meant that everyone remembered the summers in Largs as always being tropically warm. Largs is also the gateway to the other nostalgic destination, Millport, on the Little Cumbrae Isle. Bicycle rides around the little island were another treasured childhood memory for many and I was no different.

I left the Ducati opposite the newly refurbished, re-opened Nardini's Cafe Restaurant and Ice Cream Parlour. It is one of the most beautiful Art Deco buildings in Scotland and the owners have returned it to its full 1930's glory with brilliant white rendered accentuated by coloured neon lights. Inside the traditional art deco touches were still there, as were the wicker chairs that were a signature of the old place.

I sat down and a pretty young waitress came to take my order. I ordered a cappuccino with a Danish pastry. While I waited, I admired the superbly sympathetic redecoration, from the octagonal lights, through the sunburst design on the glass to the sumptuous carpet; I realised that Humphrey Bogart's Marlowe would feel right at home in this treasure from a different age.

When the coffee and the pastry arrived I savoured them, enjoying the strong but smooth blend of espresso bean with the indulgent sweetness of the Danish. All too soon it was time to leave and I promised myself that it wouldn't be so long until my next visit.

I was back in Wemyss Bay at five to four and I pulled into Leapmoor Road with a couple of minutes to spare. The road was close to the waterfront with a stunning vista across the Forth of Clyde to Dunoon and Rothesay. I imagined that it would be spectacular on a fine summer's day but today the sun had set and what I could see of the Firth was blanketed in a low lying mist that restricted visibility to a couple of hundred yards.

The Callaghan house was on the river side of the street and was like the rest of the houses, a relatively new looking building with four or five bedrooms. Although it was decorated in a similar white render, it had none of the charm or distinctiveness of the cafe I had just visited. The garden was well tended and tidy but being December there wasn't much in the way of colour. There was a double garage off to the right of the house and I parked the bike on the gravel drive in front of it.

I crunched the gravel underfoot as I walked to the front door and as I was about to ring the bell, the door opened. A lady in her early sixties stood in the portal, Mrs. Callaghan I presumed. She was extremely thin with the pale complexion of a Celtic ancestry. Her hair was the colour of ripened wheat, shot through with grey, styled in a perm that lifted it from her face. Her brown eyes were wide and saddled with deep grey bags that indicated someone who wasn't sleeping well. She opened her mouth with its row of bleached white dentures, "Mr. Campbell."

I nodded agreement, "That's me,"

"I'm Eileen Callaghan. Please come in."

I entered the house, into an expansive hall with a stair leading directly from the door. A simple chandelier of lights hung from the second floor ceiling above the bottom of the stair and created a striking introduction to the house.

"You have a lovely home, Mrs. Callaghan," I stated to give my mouth something to do.

"Thank you. Joe inherited some money last year and we decided to use that along with his lump sum from work to buy this place. I think it's too big but he wanted to be right on the shore. It hasn't worked out exactly as we hoped."

"Oh why is that?" I asked as I walked behind her.

"Joe had a stroke back in March. I would hope that you won't stress him too much, Mr. Campbell."

"I'm sorry to hear that. I'm only trying to get an impression of how things were in the office before Rory died, I'll try not to cause any upset."

We walked through a living room and dining room before she guided me into a conservatory. Joe Callaghan was sitting in a high-backed armchair facing out onto the river. He looked to be a beanpole of a man from what I could see. He filled the length of the seat and his legs stretched out before him, resting on a stool. He turned as we entered and I noticed that he seemed to have some paralysis down the left side of his face and body.

"Joe, this is Mr. Campbell. He's the man I told you was coming to visit you."

"'ello." Joe's speech was distorted and if I hadn't been expecting the word I might not have recognised it.

Mrs. Callaghan pointed to another chair and told me to have a seat. "I'll get us some tea," she said.

I removed the digital recorder from under my leathers and placed it on the coffee table.

"I hope you don't mind me recording our conversation, Mr Callaghan."

He indicated his assent with a nod of his head while gesturing with his right hand.

"I wanted to talk to you about Rory Kilpatrick. Do you remember Rory?"

"Yesss. Shame wit' happened tae 'im." His words were slurred and practically inaudible.

"What do you remember about him?"

"Wis a goo' lad, 'oo goo' sometimes"

"Why was that?"

"Would't take whit wis comin' tae him, would't dae as he wis tellt." He said as forcefully as he could which caused a drop of saliva to escape and dribble on to his shirt. Mrs. Callaghan was back with a pot of tea, three china cups and a plate of cakes on a tray which she laid on the coffee table. She picked up a tissue from a shelf that ran around the outside of the conservatory; she gentled wiped the spittle from Mr. Callaghan's face and shirt. I looked at the family pictures that decorated the shelf; Joe a much bigger, indeed giant of a man. He was well over six feet tall with broad shoulders and a barrel of a chest, full of life and vitality. I looked at him now and saw someone robbed of much of what he once was. There were pictures of children, grand-children and one of the Callaghans on their wedding day.

The tea was poured and I began the interview again.

"Did you get on well with him?"

"Maist o' the time."

"Did he cause problems?"

"'Ready tellt ye. Would't dae as wis tellt." The frustration of trying to communicate, allied with my inability to understand was obviously angering him.

"Calm down, Joe. You know what the doctor said."

"I'm sorry Mr. Callaghan. I didn't mean to upset you." He struggled to lift the cup of tea to his mouth with his good hand.

"Sawright, ma fault."

"Do you remember the night that Rory died? The night of the Christmas party."

"Cannae 'emember whit happened." He shook his head.

"Do you know what happened to Rory?"

"Train killt him. Should ha' do' whit he wis tellt."

"Is there anything you can tell me about the work you were doing in the run up to his death?"

"Wis si'ple. Nothing 'omplicated aboot it."

I began to think that I wasn't going to get any more from him. He appeared to regret something between Rory and himself but was either unwilling or unable to articulate what the big discord was.

"Do you think anyone would know?"

"Pals, 'ey did as 'ey were tellt."

"His mates, they knew?"

"An' Maloney. 'e knows every'ing."

"Who is Maloney?"

Quietly he said more to himself than to me, "Should ha' do' whit he wis tellt."

Mrs. Callaghan intervened, "I'm sorry Mr Campbell but I think that's enough, he gets tired very quickly these days."

"Yes, I understand." I finished my tea chatting with Mrs. Callaghan about living on the coast, the town and the new Nardini's.

I packed my recorder away and Mrs. Callaghan walked me to the door.

"When did you move in?" I asked.

"February. A month before his stroke."

"Thanks for your time, Mrs. Callaghan and give your husband my thanks also."

"He wasn't much help was he?"

"Not particularly but I'll keep plugging away. Good-bye Mrs. Callaghan."

"Good-bye Mr. Campbell." I shook her hand and walked back to the bike. She watched me until I had pulled out of the drive on to the road, she waved as I left.

I rode the bike pretty fast all the way up until the usual tailback from the Kingston Bridge. I felt as thwarted in the investigation as I was on the road. I seemed to make one step forward and then two back. I believed that there was something about Rory's office that held the key but the fates were conspiring against me, placing barriers in my path. I would have never bothered talking to Callaghan if I'd known about his stroke. I needed to get some more names from somewhere to help me progress it. I wondered if Maloney was another member of staff. I had no idea who he was but at least it was a name.

When I finished weaving my way through the traffic on Europe's busiest stretch of road, the stretch that spanned the Clyde and was known as the Kingston Bridge, I turned for Partick and my flat. I would leave my bike there again as it was impossible to park in front of Li's. The police tape was gone from the close, I hoped they had found something that would help. I stopped at an off-licence and bought six bottles of Kopparberg, some Kronenbourg for Li and two cans of Pringles.

I got into the flat, threw off my leathers and popped a bottle of cider, poured it into a long glass with loads of ice and opened both cans of Pringles. I switched on Li's substantial forty two inch plasma TV and selected the Simpsons from the Sky TV Guide.

I then switched off my brain and spent the rest of the night letting the cider, snacks and Homer divert me from my concerns and problems.

Chapter Nine

Thursday morning, I drove the ageing Civic into Buchanan Galleries, wrestling with the gear box and clutch the whole way. I found a space on the sixth floor of an extremely busy car park, among the SUVs and family hatchbacks of the mad rush of Christmas shoppers. The economic difficulties meant that many people had held out until the last minute in the hope of picking up some bargains. The newspapers were full of stories of the dismal Christmas the high street was having but Glaswegians seemed to be out in force.

It is a short walk down Glasgow's prime shopping street from the modern mall to St. Vincent Street. I arrived at almost twelve on the dot but there was no one waiting. It was a bright, crisp winter's day, the last before Christmas according to the forecast. Snow and bitter temperatures would be the order of the day from tomorrow. I watched the people hurrying passed, wrapped against the cold but walking tall, enjoying the bright sunshine. Wet weather always made people shrink as they huddled under umbrellas or hoods, their heads bent against the elements but a dry, sunny day seemed to make them reach to the sky like young seedlings.

A short, stout woman approached me along St. Vincent Street. I reckoned she was in her mid-forties, with a round face covered in heavy make-up. Her hair was coloured a bright terracotta brown with streaks of blonde and darker browns. She wore a pair of trendy, designer glasses with a black and white frame. Her coat was a cerulean blue with matching shoes and a lighter blue Radley bag, it's distinctive Scottie dog logo dangled from the handle. The coat was stretched by a considerable bosom, the buttons straining to stop the coat falling open.

"Craig?" she asked as she arrived.

"And you must be Audrey. Do you want to go somewhere for lunch?"

"Thanks, what about Caffe Nero?"

"OK," There was a franchise about 100 yards away from where we met.

We started walking towards the coffee shop, leaving behind Buchanan Street and its expensive temples to the designer gods. She walked with short, quick strides and moved her hands a lot as she spoke in a rapid fire of words that was achieved with little effort or time for a breath.

"I know that my reaction yesterday seems a bit extreme but David Stone told everybody you were looking into Rory's death and to be honest, I've been suspicious from the start." The almost gleeful tone of her voice put me on alert.

She was a gossip and this was probably the most interesting thing to happen to her in a long time.

"I need some details, I hope you'll be able to help me."

"I'll try."

We picked up some coffee and sandwiches. After stopping to add sugar to Audrey's coffee, we found a table at the back of the cafe.

"Audrey, I'd like you tell me a bit about Derek Norman."

She shivered involuntarily, "Davie said you wanted to talk about him. He's horrible, there's something slimy about him."

"Have you had problems with him?"

"Not as bad as one or two others but he's got no understanding of personal space." She made a slurping noise as she drank.

"Did he touch you?"

"Occasionally, he puts his hand on you when he's talking to you but it's the fact he stands so close, it's very intimidating. And the smell, oh it's disgusting, like an old sewer." Her face contorted, the heavy foundation make-up cracked at the edges of her eyes. I had the strange and uncharitable thought that she looked like a drag queen.

"Has anybody raised complaints with your Human Resources department?"

"I think one girl did, but he got out of it by saying how sorry he was and how it wouldn't happen again. It's difficult because some guys could do the same thing and you wouldn't mind but there's just something about him that makes it creepier. Do you know what I mean?"

"I think I understand. Do you know if he is into body building in a big way or does he just work out?"

"I'm not sure but I think I've seen him with some of that protein supplement stuff you can get from fitness shops, but I don't think he competes or anything. I've never taken too much interest to be honest."

"Do you remember the disagreement with Rory over Isabel's picture?"

She gasped,"Oh that was horrible wasn't it. Rory was furious." Her tone of voice denied that she thought it was horrible, instead it took on the relish of someone enjoying a really juicy piece of scandal.

"Davie said that there was an argument after a meeting, do you know if that was the end of it?"

"It upset Rory, I don't think he was a man that enjoyed arguments but after it he couldn't look the road Norman was on, never mind speak to him."

"Someone I spoke to said he saw Rory with a large guy and another man the night he was killed. Does Norman have any friends who could have helped him?"

"Not in the office, that's for sure. He might have away from work. Do you think he could have killed Rory? Oh that's terrible."

"I'm not saying that, I'm trying to understand what might have happened." I decided to steer the conversation on to a safer path. "What about Brian Swanson, what kind of guy was he?"

"He was nice enough, I suppose, but he was a bit of a chancer. He was into gambling in a big way. At lunch time, if he wasn't in the bookies, he'd be in an internet cafe playing online poker."

"Was he in financial difficulty?" My experience with insurance cases had taught me that excessive gambling could lead people to do things they would never have considered otherwise.

"Sorry, I don't know."

"Did he ever have a run in with Norman?"

Her faced wrinkled, the make-up crumbling again as she tried to remember, "Oh yes, there was something. Brian thought he was a comedian. He and one of the IT guys changed the wallpaper on Norman's computer. They found a picture of some guy in a pair of Calvin Klein's, signed it 'To Derek, all my love Clive' and made it the background for his computer. Norman went nuts, he complained to HR and the IT guy was suspended, Brian got an official warning. It was Brian's idea and Norman was screaming at him, he would kill him if he ever did anything like that again. It was a wee bit funny and a big bit scary."

"Norman does seem to have a very short fuse, do you think that's why he left England?"

"I don't know but it's a possibility."

"Is there anything else you can tell me about the office that might have something to do with Rory's death?"

She continued to slurp on her latte as we spoke, it was a distraction I could have done without.

"I don't know about his death but he seemed to have fallen out with Joe Callaghan, his boss."

"I met Mr. Callaghan last night. He seemed to be uncomfortable with our discussion."

"I'm not sure what it was about but they had an argument a couple of weeks before Rory died. Brian would have been able to tell you, he was at a meeting with Rory and Mr C. Anyway, whatever it was, things were very strained between them after it."

"Was there ever any problem between them before that?"

"Nothing serious. Rory was very dedicated to doing things properly. He would speak up at staff meetings against things he thought weren't being done correctly, Mr Callaghan couldn't be bothered with it sometimes."

"Would you say that Rory was a trouble maker at work?"

"No, no, nothing like that. He was just someone who didn't like to accept something he thought wasn't right."

"Do you remember much about the night that Rory died? The party I mean."

"Well, to be honest with you not much, I was blootered that night, what a hangover I had the next day." Her tone seemed inappropriate again and I wondered about the face she portrayed to the world. There was something very artificial about it.

"Is there anything else you can think of that might help me?"

"I can't think of anything but I'll let you know." She leaned over and touched my hand. I did well not to withdraw it as a shiver of revulsion ran through me. There was a lot about this woman that I didn't like and I had to remember to take everything she said cautiously, I wasn't convinced that there wasn't at least a degree of exaggeration in everything she said.

She spent the rest of our time together quizzing me about my love life with all the subtlety of a Guantanamo Bay investigator. I parried her questions, trying to divert the conversation but she was persistent. When we had finished our lunch, I was glad when she said that she had to get back to work. I gave her my card and told her to call me anytime, she said she would and we parted.

I walked back up Buchanan Street leaving Audrey to walk back to her office. I looked in some shop windows as I strolled. I still didn't have anything for my mother or anybody else for that matter but my heart wasn't in it and I arrived at the car empty handed.

I drove the mile and a bit to my office, cursing the awkward gearbox of Li's "classic" car.

The office was in the same state of ordered disrepair I had left it, with the neatly stacked boxes of paper a counterpoint to the broken furniture. I began moving the boxes out from the office to the boot of the car. After two trips I noticed a brown envelope behind the door that I had missed on my previous visit. My name was printed on a white label stuck to the front. I opened it and removed a white sheet of standard photocopier paper. Laser printed type told me in a large bold font, Stop sticking your nose in or the next time it won't be your office that gets damaged, it'll be your face. There were no other marks and not surprisingly the author had forgotten to sign it.

After what happened to Mrs. Capaldi I was in no mood to be intimated by this person but the deeper I dug the more I realised how dangerous this could be.

I finished the transfer of the documents to the car and sat in the office with my legitimate mail. There was nothing urgent, I had already found the information that the insurance company requested. I called the police station in Partick to let them know about the threatening letter.

I was patched through to the incident room and spoke to DC Cooper, "Hello, Detective. I'm at my office and I found a letter I didn't notice on Tuesday when I was here. Let's say that the author isn't sending me Christmas wishes."

"A threat?"

"Yes."

"Can you bring it in today?"

"Yes, I'll come in on my way home. I shouldn't be too long."

"That's fine. I'm in the modular building in the car park. There's not enough space in the main building for all the extra officers."

"OK. I'll see you soon."

I finished tearing up the junk mail, locked the office and drove to Partick.

*

A portable office that functioned as the incident room occupied four of the car parking spaces and restricted access to others. I drove round the small area and out again. It was another ten minutes before I found a parking space further along Dumbarton Road. I walked back to the station, a sergeant at the desk directed me to the temporary accommodation when I asked to speak to DC Cooper, after he called to confirm that she would be willing to talk to me.

I knocked on the door of the modular building and opened it when I heard someone shouting an invitation to enter.

DC Cooper was sitting to the left of the door at a cramped desk and she greeted me warmly when she saw me. "Mr. Campbell, good to see you, please come in and have a seat. This is our home for the moment. Over there is the data input area, where all the statements that the boys and girls on the ground collect are put into the HOLMES system. This is where the detectives try and make sense of it all." As she spoke she pointed to the areas she was referring to. It seemed a ridiculously small area for the number of desks that were shoehorned into it.

The detectives' area featured a large white board with a variety of information written on or pinned to it. It included photographs of my flat and the stairwell. I caught my breath at the sight of a photograph of Mrs. Capaldi in the hospital bed.

"Did you bring the envelope?"

"Yes." I handed the envelope over inside the plastic sleeve that I had placed it in before I set off from the office.

"That's great, we'll check for fingerprints and send it to the lab to see if there's anything they can tell us. I'm afraid it may take a few days. We don't have the resources of the American TV shows, unfortunately."

"Have you found anything that might help?" I asked.

"To be honest, in a case like this it's hard to know what is forensic evidence and what's not. We found some fingerprints that aren't yours or Mrs. Capaldi's, but we would need to know who has been in your flat recently and then get their prints to eliminate them. It's the same with trace evidence, it might easily be from friends rather than from the perpetrator."

I took out my notepad, made a list of my friends and my landlord with their relevant phone numbers before passing it to the detective. At that moment the door opened and middle-aged man in a navy blue suit stepped into the room.

"Sir, this is Mr. Campbell, he's the gentleman that lives in the flat that was broken into. Mr. Campbell this is DCI Munro, he's the officer leading the investigation."

I stood up and shook the detective's hand; his grip was firm, a proper man's handshake. "It's nice to meet you Mr. Campbell, I'm only sorry it's under these terrible circumstances. I believe you were very close to Mrs. Capaldi."

"Yes, she was a special neighbour and friend."

He was about five feet eleven inches tall, slim and athletic looking for his age. He sported a thick moustache that I guess he had worn since the late seventies or early eighties. It was brown shot through with grey, but less so than the hair on his head which was nearly white. His face was creased and wrinkled, prematurely aged, probably from smoking as I caught a faint whiff of cigarette smoke drifting over from him. His suit looked like it had been dry cleaned beyond the safe limit for the material, his shirt was less than perfectly ironed and I noticed the white band on his wedding ring finger that indicated a recent divorce.

"We're doing everything we can to catch the guy who did this," he said as if to reassure me.

"I understand that."

"Is there anything else you can add to your original statement?"

"I've just brought in a letter I received from an anonymous admirer that was left in my office."

"That's right, I remember someone saying that your office had been done as well. May I?" He indicated the letter to DC Cooper. She passed the plastic wallet to her commanding officer along with a box containing disposable rubber gloves. He removed a pair from the box, slipped them over his hands before he reached into the wallet to remove the envelope. He read the note and inspected both sides before putting it carefully back in the wallet.

"Less than subtle, I would say." He snapped off the gloves and dropped them into a bin.

"Hopefully we'll get something from it," DC Cooper added.

"I hope you're following my DC's advice, Mr. Campbell. We don't want another victim, do we?"

"Well, I know I certainly don't," I replied with a smile. He seemed to think that was a positive reply and didn't follow up his question.

DC Cooper took up the dialogue, "We've had the post-mortem report back for Mrs. Capaldi."

"What did it say?" I asked.

"Well there is no sign of any other violence, so I don't think she suffered other than the fall. It could be that whoever it was, knocked her over as he was trying to get away."

There was little comfort in her words, whoever it was shouldn't have been in my flat, shouldn't have knocked my friend down and shouldn't have killed her. It didn't change my resolve to hunt them down and make sure he or she was punished.

"OK, thanks for letting me know. When will I be able to get back into my flat?"

"The scene of crime techs should be finished early tomorrow, you should be able to get back in sometime in the afternoon. You'll need a locksmith as the inside door still isn't fixed, we've been locking the outside door to keep the place secure but it's better for you if they are both locked."

"I forgot about that, thanks. I'll speak to the guy who sorted the office for me. Is there anything else?"

She looked to her boss, who shook his head, "Nothing at the moment, Mr Campbell. We'll keep you informed of any developments."

I shook their hands and weaved my way through the cramped room to the door. Outside the clouds blocked the sun and the temperature seemed to be dropping again, the air smelled of snow. I walked back to the car and drove back to Li's place.

*

After brewing a much needed coffee, I was back on the phone. I called "Boab" the locksmith and asked him to come to the flat the following day at about four o'clock.

"Yir no' huvin' much luck, son, ur ye?" was his response. He agreed he would be come the following day.

The next person I called was Carol.

"Hi, Craig." Her voice was bubbly and she sounded pleased to hear from me.

"Hi Carol, how are you?"

"I'm fine but it doesn't sound as if you are." A note of disquiet was discernible now.

"It's been a tough week, my office and flat were broken into. My elderly neighbour was killed in a fall when she went to see what was going on in the flat, she fractured her skull and never recovered."

"Oh God, Craig. I don't know what to say."

"There's not much anyone can say. I'm still kind of in shock myself."

"What happened with the office and the flat?"

"I've been working on a case, the death of a young guy last year."

"Is this for an insurance company?"

"No, it's for the lad's mother. He died on railway tracks when a train hit him; it appeared he was drunk but from what I have discovered it's looking more like murder. I think that's why the flat and office were broken into, they were looking for evidence."

"Oh Craig, is there anything I can do?"

"I don't think so, it was just to let you know that I might not be able to take you for that run on the bike."

"I understand, that's no problem. Tell you what why don't I come round on Saturday and give you a hand with the flat?"

"Are you sure?"

"Yes. I would like to help after you helped me with that uncle of mine."

"How is the old grouch, anyway? Recovered from the shock of having to give in to you?"

She laughed. "Just about. He's harmless really."

"I'll see you on Saturday, I'm in Chancellor Street just off Byres Road."

"OK see you then. Look after yourself."

"I will, bye."

I decided to take my mind off things by doing a bit of cooking. I searched Li's kitchen for some ingredients and found enough for a chicken and bacon risotto. The task of preparing the food was what I need to alleviate some of the pressure that seemed to be consuming me. The smell of the onions, bacon and chicken made my mouth water as I gently fried them before adding the herbs. I made a stock before I started on the rice. Half an hour later the food was ready, and I put my food on a plate making sure there was enough for Li.

I sat down with my risotto and a glass of sparkling water that I found in Li's fridge, I switched on the TV and watched an episode of X-Files that was being repeated on some channel or other. Mulder and Scully were wrestling with the problem of the alien that had taken over Krycek. I hadn't seen this episode in a while and I struggled to remember where in the long story arc of the series that this plot belonged.

We had decided not to got to the pub for the quiz night as Li was working late. The arrangements were made by text, Barry and Paul were going to come to Li's place and we would kick back on the PS3, behaving like the children we are at heart. Although I didn't see Barry and Paul as often as Li, I enjoyed their company and I was looking forward to our last get together before Christmas.

Li arrived home at seven, looking tired. The long hours of the past couple of weeks were taking his toll on him.

"Dinner's ready." I said as he walked into the living room.

"Good, what is it?"

"A risotto."

"Magic, let me at it, I'm starving."

I reheated the risotto in the microwave and Li tucked in to it with some relish.

'How did you get on today?" he asked when the meal was finished.

I told him about my meeting with Audrey Bruce.

"She sounds like a charmer."

"Tell me about it."

"The office is the key to this isn't it." He echoed my own thoughts.

"I've thought that for a while and the more I hear the stronger that belief becomes. Even if Ms. Bruce might not be the most reliable source."

I continued to detail my day, including my love letter, the visit to the police and the news that he would be rid of me the following day.

"That's not a problem, mate. You know you're welcome to stay as long as you need to."

"I'm grateful but I'll be glad to get back to my own place."

"Look Craig, I think you've got to think about your own safety. How are you going to deal with these guys if they come after you?"

"I know. It's been a while but hopefully I'll remember some Tae Kwon Do if I need it."

"How long is it since you've done any?"

"Not since the bike accident."

"It might be worth a visit to a club to refresh the skills. Is there anybody from your uni days that you could practice with?"

"Strangely enough Alex, she was in the club at uni and she's a couple of levels above me. She's a black belt, 3rd Dan; I'm a 1st Dan or at least I was. You're right, it'll kill two birds as I have to speak to her about the second alleged accident."

"Good, that should help you to take care of yourself. I wouldn't want you getting injured by a girl, you know what a baby you are." He smiled but once again there was little enthusiasm.

"Aye, you're a bloody comedian."

Barry and Paul arrived at half past seven, weighed down by a carry out from the local off sales.

"Hi Craig, how you doing?" Barry asked as he walked in.

"Hi Craig, sorry to hear about Mrs. Capaldi. She was a cracking lady."

"Thanks, I'm still a bit numb to be honest. I don't know how Lou and Maria will be coping," I replied.

"Barry, would you take a look at the netbook I found?"

"Sure, what do you need?"

"There's a password on it, I think it needs your hacking abilities."

He rooted around in his jacket pocket and pulled out a key ring with a USB data stick attached.

"I've got the very thing, right here."

"I knew you would."

The guys got themselves settled, we talked some more about what happened to Mrs. Capaldi and the investigation. Barry and Paul also thought that refreshing my defence skills would be helpful and without saying so outright, they showed their anxiety. The same doubts had begun to creep into my thoughts but that didn't change my resolve; I wouldn't be scared off by the scum bag.

"Barry, do you want a look at this computer now?"

"No problem, I'll do anything you need, mate, if it helps put these bastards away."

I went to get my rucksack from the hall while Li and Paul powered up the games console. Barry was sitting at the dining room table waiting for my return.

"I've not had a chance to get my hands on one of these before," he said as he removed the tiny computer from its box.

I watched him as he plugged the computer in and got to work. He accessed the computer bios and set an option that allowed the computer to boot from a USB device. He plugged in the USB data stick and restarted the machine. The computer then booted into a version of Linux that I wasn't familiar with. He then used a tool of his own design to extract both the account details and passwords on the machine.

As he worked, I thought about how unbelievably intelligent my friend is. He has an IQ of 198, two PHds; one in physics and the other in applied mathematics. He teaches the latter at Strathclyde University and occasionally works as a consultant for a blue chip electronics firm. A lot of people who are as bright as Barry are, for want of a better word, geeks; they struggle to interact with lesser mortals. Barry is the opposite, he is warm, friendly and sociable; there is never any hint of arrogance or snobbery. He is also very generous with his knowledge, even if he leaves his less gifted friends dumbfounded at its depth, losing us in an enthusiastic typhoon of information. He has an interest in everything, can talk intelligently and articulately on anything from sport to art. He is a top bloke and I'm glad to know him.

After about forty minutes, when the silence was only disturbed by the shouts of Li and Paul, as their virtual football matches ebbed and flowed, Barry said, "Got it."

The computer was rebooted again and this time was allowed to boot in to its native operating system. Barry entered the account and password that he had taken note of.

"Rory was obviously keen to stop anyone getting into this. He had a twelve character login and a sixteen character password."

"Good, it looks like we might be getting somewhere then."

The distinctive Ubuntu brown desktop was covered in folders, each with a date as the name. I clicked on the icon for the first date which was 1st August 2008. The folder opened into the standard file structure window and showed a list of over 200 files with a variety of titles. I checked some of the other dated folders on the desktop and found similar lists of files. It looked like a series of files relating to contract tenders. I opened a few of the files at random, some of them were written in indecipherable legalese, others had red notation that I presumed were added by Rory. It would take some time to make any sense of them and I decided to leave it until tomorrow.

I then had a look at the e-mail client, Evolution Mail. Rory had created a separate mail account from the one on his home PC. The e-mails were all sent from his work mail account and looked to copies of various pieces of correspondence sent internally and from outside parties to people in the office. I checked the last mails in the account, one from Joe Callaghan sent to Rory three days from his death.

Rory,

I would advise you to forget about this. It's not worth it.

Joe

There was no subject matter but I was pretty sure that I would be able to decipher its meaning from the rest of the mail and the documents on the computer.

Barry looked over my shoulder at the mail, "That's a veiled threat if ever I saw one. Do you think Callaghan's behind the murder?"

"Maybe, but I'm going to have to plough through the information that Rory saved here. It's definitely something to do with the PPP tenders. From the notation I've seen in the documents I've looked at so far, Rory was checking on discrepancies between the original submissions and the final documents used in the decision making."

"It smells bad."

"You're not kidding."

I changed the password on the account before I shut the computer down and packed it away in the box, returning it to the rucksack. I knew I couldn't risk letting it out of my sight.

I joined the others in front of the TV but I wasn't really interested in the games and became a pensive spectator until Barry and Paul left just before midnight. The next day would be a busy one.

Chapter Ten

Friday the 18th of December dawned cold with a hint of snow in the air. I ran through the same stretching routine I had used the previous morning to work out the stiffness in my joints. I was glad that I would be sleeping in my own bed that night.

After a quick breakfast, I called Alex. "Hi, Alex"

"Craig, how's things?"

"Busy. I was looking for a favour."

"Another one, you're using up your allocation rapidly."

"Are you still doing Tae Kwon Do?"

"When I get a chance. It's not too easy with the job. There's a couple of guys on the force that are pretty good and I spar with them occasionally."

"I need a refresher. I've not done anything since I had my bike accident and I'm worried that after everything that's happened, I might need to protect myself."

Her voice was stern again, "I'd rather you backed off and let us handle it."

"I know, but even if I do, I'm still worried that whoever is behind this might come after me."

"OK. Are you free this morning?" I asked hopefully.

"Yes."

"There's a place in Anderston, the Eastern Martial Arts centre, do you know it?"

"I think so, it's in a converted church?"

"That's the one. Meet me there at half nine, I know the owner and he'll let us spar there."

"Have you got a spare suit?"

"I'll bring it with me. See you soon."

*

A short trip along Argyle Street brought me to the centre five minutes early. It was housed in an Edwardian church, sold by the Church of Scotland, like so many others, as church attendance began to fall in the early eighties. The redevelopment had left the shell of the building intact, the design reflected the simpler architectural style of its time. Inside there was a small reception area, bright and spacious with pictures of various Tae Kwon Do bouts. In a small recess, there was a large stone statue of a Korean Buddha, sitting serenely in the lotus position.

I was admiring the statue when a man walked through the internal door. "Hello, can I help you?"

"I'm here for a sparring session with Alex Menzies."

"Oh hi, I'm Bill Carroll. I run this place."

I shook the hand he extended towards me. "Craig Campbell."

"How long have you been a Tae Kwon Do player?"

"I started when I was eight but I've been away from it for three years; I had an accident on my motorbike and hurt my shoulder."

"So what brings you back?"

"I thought I could do with the exercise and thought I would see if I could still remember what I was taught." I didn't think he needed to know that I might be a target for someone with violent intentions.

"What level did you reach?"

"1st Dan"

"Well there's an advanced class here on Tuesdays and Thursdays at 9:00 pm if you fancy coming along after New Year."

"I might take you up on that, thanks Bill."

Alex arrived carrying a large bag.

"Morning Bill, thanks for letting us use the hall."

"No problem, Alex. Any time. I'll let you get on."

She looked fantastic. Her hair was shorter than I remembered, her natural light brown colour was tinted with subtle blonde highlights. Her duck blue eyes shone with vivacity. She was dressed in a black woollen coat, over a white shirt and blue jeans. She carried a pink sports bag over her shoulder.

Memories of our time together flooded in to my mind as she walked over, gave me a platonic hug and a chaste kiss on the cheek. "It's been too long, Mr. Campbell."

"I know. Thanks for all your help with this Alex."

We walked through the internal door into a short corridor. We turned right into another longer corridor with doors on either side. I walked into the gents changing room on the right while Alex turned left into the ladies. The room was like any other you would see in gyms and leisure centres around the world. There were lockers lining the wall with bench seats in the middle of the room. The seats were divided along their length by a pole lined with hooks to hang clothes on. The smell was that of sweat, deodorant and after shave. The showers were through at the back of the room on the left.

I stored my clothes, helmet and the valuable rucksack in one of the lockers. I changed into the suit and picked up the protective helmet Alex had supplied me with, she said that the other pads were in the hall.

When I was ready I went back out into the corridor and turned right towards the main hall. You could tell by the shape of the windows and the roof space what the building had been used for but that was the only clue. The floor was dominated by a large mat at its centre, with the equipment on the walls at the side. At the far end of the room, where the altar would have been in the church, a huge Yin/Yang symbol was painted on the wall.

Before starting any serious sparring we sat in silent meditation to help improve our breathing and blood flow, it also helped to bring an inner calm in preparation for the exercise ahead. We then helped each other into our padding to cover our chest and stomach.

As we padded up I asked Alex about Brian Swanson's accident.

"I looked at the accident report and there doesn't seem to be any doubts. The only strange thing is that he wasn't wearing a seat belt but there are still people who refuse to wear one."

"Did any one ask if he was in the habit of driving without one?"

"His family and friends weren't sure."

"Hopefully, it's just a coincidence then." My concerns about Swanson hadn't been assuaged as much as I had hoped.

When we were fully armoured, we started our sparring slowly, the combination of Alex' superior skill and my rustiness meant that I took far more blows than I gave her. She talked me through the moves and gradually I began to find a rhythm that felt natural. Although I knew I was well short of being able to go into a proper match, there were signs that I had not forgotten everything I had ever learned.

We sparred for about an hour, by the end of the session I was doused in sweat and feeling an ache in my muscles.

"You've done OK, Craig." Alex said as we removed the padding.

"I'm exhausted but I enjoyed it, it felt good. I think I should take Bill up on his offer and come regularly."

"Aye, particularly if you're intent in noising up some bad people." The lightness of her tone wasn't reflected in her expression.

She took a drink from a bottle of water she had bought with her and handed it to me.

"You know that you need to be licensed these days to be a private detective?" she asked pointedly.

"I'm not planning on make a career out of it, honest. I'm helping Mrs Kilpatrick but most of all I want to know who killed Mrs Capaldi, she was a friend."

"I understand that, Craig, but the risks you're taking are crazy." She touched my arm as she spoke.

I thought I would take the opportunity to get the answer to something that had bothered me for a while. "Alex, did you ever have strong feelings for me?"

She withdrew her hand and gave me a quizzical look, "Of course, as a mate."

"Never anything more?"

She look uncomfortable as she replied, "Sorry, but no. The sex was great, we had a few laughs and you were good company but I didn't need anything more. I take it that wasn't the case for you."

I paused as I considered my answer, "No, I thought I loved you."

Her face fell. "I'm sorry Craig, I didn't mean to hurt you, I didn't realise. I thought you were looking for the same thing as I was from the relationship. Why didn't you say something?"

"I don't know, to be honest. I probably thought you would feel the same some day and say something to me. I'm a Scottish male after all," I said to lighten the mood.

"Maybe it's better that you didn't say something, it would have put a strain on things."

"What about Andrew, are you two serious?"

"Yeah, I think we are. We've been going out for two years and living together for just over a year. He's a great guy and I love him. What about you?"

"Nothing serious since we split. I met someone recently and we'll see how that develops."

The conversation tailed off into an awkward silence, so we headed to the changing rooms.

I showered and changed, thanked Alex at the door of the centre and she went back home to get ready for her shift later that day. As I walked to the Ducati, I switched my phone on. There was a voice mail from DC Cooper to say that the flat would be free at one o'clock. It was 11:30, so I had time for lunch.

I rode the bike back along Argyle Street and parked close to Beanscene, opposite the Kelvingrove Art Gallery and Museum. The mix of great coffee, good food and a diverse range of music makes the cafe an excellent place to spend a lunchtime. I ordered a panini with roasted Mediterranean vegetables and feta cheese. The food and coffee restored my energies levels after the exhausting exercise of the morning.

The time in the cafe gave me some time to observe the world. A young couple arrived and sat at the table next to me. They had a very small baby with them and they moved with the extreme care of new parents everywhere. The father was particularly careful as he removed the little boy from his warm travel suit, while the mother prepared to sit and feed the baby. The parents looked both elated and exhausted, the baby looked content.

In one corner, a couple of tourists were talking in animated Italian, their arms and hands communicating as much as their lips. I thought of Mrs. Capaldi and I felt my eyes welling up. I blinked the tears away.

I took my notebook out of my rucksack. I jotted down some things that I still needed to check. At the top of the list was Derek Norman, the mystery man. I decided to try and get hold of him before going to see Callaghan again that night. I finished my lunch and waved my thanks to the staff. Outside a mixture of hail and snow was falling, beginning to lie on the grass in front of the museum.

Fully revived, I walked back to the bike and began the brief trip to Chancellor Street and home. After finding a space for the Ducati I searched for my keys in my leathers. I opened the close door, as I passed, the door to Mrs. Capaldi's flat opened and I instantly turned expecting to see her friendly face or to hear the hint of mischief in her voice. Instead it was Lou, looking drawn and spent, as if the grief was ripping at his soul.

"Oh hello, Craig."

"Hi, Lou."

"Are you getting back into the flat?"

"Yes, how are things with you?"

"Hellish. You don't realise how much there is to organise for a funeral, how many people you have to tell. It can be very tiring telling the same story of what happened, even listening to other people tell it, it's like it's happening again and again." His face crumpled in sorrow.

"How's Maria doing?"

"I think she's still numb. She's in the flat with a couple of friends of mum from church. She chats away, makes tea and sandwiches for everyone that comes in but it's as if she's not really here. I'm sure it'll come crashing down on her soon."

"It affects everyone in different ways." It was a platitude but I wasn't sure what else to say. I knew how bad I felt and couldn't really imagine how much worse it was for Lou and Maria. Their mother had raised them since their father died when they were still in their teens.

I offered another cliché, "You know if there is anything I can do, just ask."

"I know Craig. I know how well you and mum got on, I appreciate the way you looked out for her. The funeral will be on Tuesday, ten o'clock at St. Simon's."

"I'll be there. I better go and have a look at the flat."

"Right, I'll see you later." He turned to exit the close and I paused to watch him walk away. He seemed stooped, the burden of emotion dragging him down.

DC Cooper was waiting for me in the flat.

"Good afternoon, Detective."

"Hi, I thought I would wait for you, make sure that everything was OK."

"Thanks."

"A couple of your friends, Barry and Paul, popped in to the station this morning and gave us their fingerprints. We still need Li Chen to come in."

"Yes, he runs his own business and he's been really busy on the run up to Christmas. I'll remind him to pop in when he can."

"I'd appreciate that. I'll leave you to get settled back in." She handed me the spare key for the flat's outside door and left.

I went through the living room door and it looked like someone had sprinkled several bags of icing sugar over every surface. A can of Mr. Sheen would rid me of the fingerprint dust. In truth the criminal had not been able to do much damage, probably due to Mrs. Capaldi's interruption. There were drawers pulled out of a cabinet, my books were scattered across the floor and there were papers everywhere but there was none of the wanton vandalism that was present in the office.

The bedroom looked untouched and I decided that a bath and change of clothes were in order. I soaked for over twenty minutes to help relax my muscles, tired after my morning work out. I dressed in a Beatles t-shirt, a pair of jeans and my ever trusty Converse trainers. I felt comfortable in my own clothes and relieved to be back in my own room.

In the living room I did a quick dust and tidy but I decided to leave the major clear up operation until the following day. When I was finished, I brewed a Brazilian Santos coffee I was given on my birthday. It wasn't as strong as the majority of the coffee I loved but it was very smooth with an earthiness to it that I really enjoyed.

With the notebook PC on the desk, I sat with my coffee and began the process of investigating the documentation, which I believed, might help me to get an understanding of Rory's death.

The first folder was dated 12th August and I thought that was as good a place to start as any. The files were copies of documents from three separate companies; they were outline proposals for the building of six primary and two secondary schools in the south east part of Glasgow. There was a basic plan of work for each school combined with some simple financial plans. Rory hadn't marked anything significant on any of the files, I assumed they were there as a foundation for what was to come. I got the impression that they were the files that were used to help eliminate some of the bidders and that these three contractors were to move forward into the next phase of the bidding process.

The next dated folder was for the 26th August. There were sub-folders for each of the three companies and around 18 documents in each folder. Each document was approximately 200 pages long. These were more detailed version of the previous submissions. There were detailed plans and timings for each school; there were safety statements and financial plans, it was pretty comprehensive. I soon realised that the majority of comments from Rory, typed in a bold red font, related to the financial information on each document. He had noted certain figures, 'Unchanged' or 'Changed by'; some of the changes were initialled with the company name but others were marked with a question mark. All the comments that featured a change were dated and I began to see a pattern I could follow through the subsequent files.

The next folder was 2nd October. More detailed information that now included full work details, risk assessments and safety statements. These appeared to be as close to the final submissions as you can get. The comments from Rory were now more precise and frequent. He questioned figures from each of the three bidders but there seemed to be two who were being altered to their detriment by the mysterious question mark. However, every change for the third firm was to their benefit. I wondered how this was possible, I thought that all bids for these kinds of contract were sealed but there was obviously some questions to be answered about the office in which Rory worked.

The final folder was dated 15th November and appeared to be the decision of the tendering committee. The same firm that had benefited from the mystery editor's ministrations had won the contract to build the schools and then, more importantly, to collect the money from the public purse for the next thirty years. The name of the company was New Future Schools, a very similar name to the one that had cropped up in my search of Rory's home PC, New Future Homes.

I booted up my own Mac and loaded the New Future Homes web site. The company was owned by Patrick Maloney and had been in existence for over 30 years. The history page informed me that Mr. Maloney had built the company from a bricklaying contractor to a builder of luxury houses and flats across Scotland. The site also mentioned the diversification into PPP building contracts. From what I could gather the move had only come with the bid for the Glasgow schools. There were three other areas that had also awarded contracts for a total of 19 schools across Scotland.

I searched a bit further and found a biography of Maloney, the creator, owner and managing director of the New Future Group as it was now calling itself.

'Patrick Maloney was born in the Gorbals area of Glasgow on 25th June, 1949. He was one of three brothers and six sisters;

they were raised in a two room tenement flat. His father, Seamus, worked in the Parkhead Forge while his wife, Doris, looked after the house and children.

Patrick left school with no qualifications but earned a place on a building apprentice scheme with Plant Builders in 1964. He worked as a bricklayer with Plant until 1972, when he set up a small firm called Maloney Trades with money he had saved. The firm grew quickly and changed its name in 1982 to New Future Homes.

Mr. Maloney has been a member of the Labour Party since 1965 and is noted for his many charitable works for the people of the East End of Glasgow.

He is married with three children, who after obtaining their degrees all returned to work with their father and have contributed to the great success of the company.'

A paragon of virtue and pillar of the community, apparently, but the picture I had of how his business was being conducted was less impressive.

I returned to the notebook to check on the e-mail account that Rory had created. The mail all seemed to be copies of internal mail from within his office. Some of it seemed unimportant, general office mail organising meetings, informing the staff of policy and procedures. I finally found a mail dated 12th November, 2008. It was a reply to a mail Rory had sent to Joe Callaghan.

'Rory,

I can find no evidence of any changes to the documents you mentioned other than those completed by the companies themselves. I am sure you are mistaken.

Cheers

Joe'

Rory's initial suspicions obviously were based on his experience rather than the specific evidence he had then amassed. There were some other mails where Rory stated his specific allegations although he didn't accuse anyone in particular. A mail dated 20th December, the day before he died.

'Mr Callaghan,

I have now compiled a dossier of the inconsistencies that have appeared during the tendering proposals for the schools in the South East of the city. I plan to use these documents to present a concise report that will be passed to the audit section and if necessary, the police. I have given you ample opportunity to do something to stop this but I feel I now have no choice but to proceed.

Yours sincerely

Rory Kilpatrick'

The reply was succinct and to the point

'Rory,

I warn you not pursue this any further, please.

Joe'

The next mail I found was one dated the same day addressed to a Andrew Turner.

'Mr. Turner,

Would it be possible to arrange a meeting to talk to you about something confidential?

Rory Kilpatrick'

The reply was an automated "out of office" message,

'I am out of the office attending a meeting in Edinburgh until Monday 22nd December. Please call my mobile number

for anything urgent.

   Andrew Turner'

I presumed that Mr. Turner was the person in the audit section that Rory wanted to pass the information to. He never got to that meeting and someone made sure that he wouldn't get the facts to anyone who could do anything about it. I couldn't believe that the fragile, shadow of a man I met in Wemyss Bay was responsible for Rory's death but the evidence was beginning to stack up against him. It seemed unlikely that he could have committed the act himself and there were other people involved in Rory's murder. I knew I would have to have a closer look at Mr. Patrick Maloney and his New Future Group.

I looked up from the computer and realised that the daylight was rapidly disappearing. I called the number for the New Future Group.

"New Future House, Claudia speaking, how may I help you?" Her voice was southern counties English, with a clipped and precise diction.

"I would like to speak to Mr. Maloney, please."

"Have you spoken to him on a previous occasion?"

"No, but this is very urgent."

"I'm sorry, Mr. Maloney will not take any calls without you first speaking to our Public Affairs Department."

"I'm pretty sure that he doesn't want anyone else hearing what I have to say."

"Well I'm very sorry, sir, but it is company policy. As you can imagine Mr. Maloney is a very busy man and can't take calls from any Tom, Dick or Harry." I could hear her climbing on her metaphorical high horse.

"That's fine. Tell him that I am neither Tom, Dick nor Harry. My name is Craig Campbell and I'm going to nail his arse to the nearest police station door." I slammed the phone down. Not my finest moment but I was frustrated at the walls that were being erected in front of me. I wondered if the guard dog would pass the message up to her master. I was hoping that she would and that it might rattle Mr. Maloney's cage. Someone from Rory's office would probably have told him I was sniffing around and my name might be enough to provoke a reaction.

The phone hadn't finished vibrating from my anger when the intercom for the close door buzzed.

"Hello"

"Hello, it's Boab tae fix yir door."

"Oh right. I'm on the first floor."

Boab was his usual talkative and opinionated self. The banking industry got both barrels, "Shower o' bankers wi' a capital W" and "Imagine puttin' a bastard greengrocer in charge of a bank," and "they don't huv tae worry about their pensions, naw they're set fur life." He continued in a similar vein the whole time that he was working on my lock. After about fifty minutes he was finished and I paid him before he left. I would sort out the insurance claims when I could get my life back to something like normality.

*

Before I could make a move on Maloney, I decided that I needed to look at Callaghan with a less sympathetic eye. I had been reluctant to give him a hard time due to his illness but if I was going to get to the truth, I needed to be tougher.

I made myself some pasta with a tomato and basil sauce from a bottle, a glass of sparkling water and an apple as dessert. When I was finished, I put the dishes in the dishwasher and gave the kitchen a clean.

As I was leaving the flat, I waved to Maria, she was looking out of Mrs. Capaldi's window with a distant look in her eye. She waved and managed a small, sad smile. I'm sure she regretted being so far from home when her mother was hurt and I could almost feel the pain that burned in her eyes.

Instead of riding straight to the M8, I took a diversion to Derek Norman's flat. He almost shut the door in my face when he opened it but the old foot in the gap worked a treat.

"Mr. Norman, I want to talk to you. I need to understand your side of the story."

"I've got nothing to say."

"Please, I'm not here to judge you."

"Come in," he said with obvious reluctance.

As I walked through the hall I noticed one of the bedroom doors was open. Inside the room was a collection of expensive looking gym equipment, a treadmill, an exercise bike and two different weight machines. I was back in the sparse living room when Norman offered me a seat.

"Mr. Norman, I'm sorry I upset you when I was here before but I need to make sense of what happened between you and Rory."

"I told you it was a misunderstanding."

"You took a photograph of his girlfriend," I prompted.

He sat down in one of the armchairs and sighed, "Yes. Have you seen her?"

I nodded.

"I don't know why I took the photograph or kept it on my phone. It was a private fantasy, I suppose. She's the kind of woman that never even looks twice at the likes of me. " He drew a circle with his hand in front of his scarred face. "This, puts off women before they even notice the smell. Yes, Mr. Campbell, I know I smell but there's nothing I can do about it. I've seen more doctors than I can remember and none of them can help me. It's a glandular problem. I've tried prescription soaps and deodorants but nothing works."

"I understand that would be a problem but it doesn't explain your behaviour towards women, you seem to have upset a few in your office."

"Christ, I can't win. I try to be friendly but I can never get it right. With the problems I have, I've always been shy, hopeless in social situations, always expecting people to judge me. When I came north I wanted to try and change that but I disgust people, women in particular."

"Why did you come to Glasgow, there are rumours that you were running from something?"

He shook his head in a mixture of resignation and annoyance. "Who the hell said that?"

"I can't say."

"I'll bet you spoke to that bitch Audrey Bruce. She's a nasty piece of work, she's never happier than when she's spreading lies. Gossip is her lifeblood and the more malicious the better." He slumped back into the armchair.

I watched him as he sat in silence. There seemed to be an air of exhaustion about him. I was about to ask him what did bring him to Scotland when he started to speak again.

"I came here for a fresh start. That's a laugh, it's been worse here than in Newcastle. Add being English to my other problems and it's ten times worse. I thought that maybe a new town, new job and new people would give me a chance to build some confidence and to make friends. I try hard to fit in but I'm not very good at it. Maybe I try too hard."

I felt a degree of sympathy at the abject figure that sat opposite me. His life appeared lonely and depressing. He didn't have the social skills needed to survive the modern world but somehow I didn't see him as a killer.

"I've heard there were two other women who you had a run in with." I coaxed him gently, waiting for the explosion.

Instead he just shook his head. "If you mean the supermarket incident that was exactly as I said it was. I had met a guy at the gym and he invited me over to his place for a bite of lunch with his girlfriend. I went into that place to get a bottle of wine, that's all. No stalking, no perversion."

He drew a deep sigh. "The girl I lost my temper with was because she laughed at me and told me she wouldn't be seen dead with the likes of me. It wasn't nice to hear but I lost the plot and was sorry for it afterwards. That's my sad story Mr. Campbell, pathetic eh?"

"I'm sorry."

I stood to leave, he looked up from the chair, "I'm sorry about Rory but I had nothing to do with it."

the money generated by the council or the government to secure his company's future. He couldn't risk not getting the contract so he wanted Joe to help him."

"What did he ask Joe to do?"

"He wanted him to monitor the other tenders, at first Joe thought that all he would be doing was making sure that Maloney's company would be in the final three but Maloney applied some more pressure and offered Joe a bribe."

"What kind of bribe?"

"You're sitting in it. I'm not sure of the details but he basically bought this house for us through some other company and then sold it to us at a discount price." Despite her obvious shame, she managed to sound detached.

"So what did Joe have to do to get the house?"

"He and some others in the office basically rigged the tender documents to favour Maloney. They worked overnight to ensure that the final tender documents were altered and reprinted by the time the committee met the following day. They used the original documents with the signatures as a template and forged the signatures on the amended papers. Joe picked people that he could trust but I don't know who they were, he wouldn't tell me, he has this strange need to feel honourable despite what has happened."

"How did Rory fit in to this?"

"Rory had worked on the initial documents and had an excellent memory. He spotted the differences and he told Joe he had evidence of what was going on."

"What did Joe do?"

"He warned Rory to keep quiet but Rory wouldn't do it; he was going to go to the auditors to get them to check out the whole tender process."

"Did Joe have anything to do with Rory's death?"

"No," she was very insistent, "not directly, that was Maloney. At least that's what Joe believed."

"Why did he think that?"

"He spoke to Maloney on the Thursday night, warning him that Rory was ready to inform the auditors. When he heard about Rory's death, he guessed what had happened." The cold detachment faltered for a moment.

"How did you find out about this?"

"The guilt was eating Joe up. He told me just before he had his stroke. The stress of his secrets was too much for him, it was probably what tipped his health over the edge."

"But he still accepted the house?"

"What else could he do? He was scared of Maloney and he didn't want to go to jail. He hoped that everyone would believe it was an accident and that would be the end of it. He's paying for his stupidity now."

"And it was the end, until I arrived."

"I knew as soon as you came here that you would find the truth, eventually."

"Why didn't you say anything?"

"I don't want him to end his life as a cripple in a prison hospital ward." She broke down and started crying.

"I'm sorry Mrs. Callaghan but a young man's life was taken from him because he wanted to do the right thing. That's my priority."

"I know."

"I'm still compiling the evidence but the police will probably want to talk to your husband."

Her sobs increased in frequency and depth. I reached over and placed my hand over her hand, she withdrew it sharply from me.

"I know that you need to do what's right but I wish you didn't. Joe's basically a good man, he just got trapped by someone he thought was a friend. I don't know what I'm going to do."

"I'm sorry."

I stood up and left her to the complex emotions she felt. The grief, guilt and shame at how her husband had behaved, competed against her love for him and the distress she felt at what would happened to them both. I could do nothing for either of them, they had already paid with Joe's ill health but there was a good chance that justice would add to their burden.

On the way back to Glasgow an idea formed in my head and instead of going straight home I went to Barry's flat in Hyndland. He was home and I asked him to do something for me and he agreed. It was a little piece of electronic wizardry and he said he would do it for me as quickly as he could, despite his doubts about the wisdom of my actions.

After my short visit I went home to a comfortable bed and slept better than I had in days.

Chapter Eleven

The next day I was up early, as I needed to get my Christmas shopping finished before Carol arrived in the afternoon. After a breakfast of muesli, scrambled eggs on toast and a cup of flavoursome Nicaraguan coffee, I travelled into the city centre.

I parked in Buchanan Galleries, one of Glasgow's more recent places of worship for those that honour the religion of retail. As it was just past nine the place was quiet for the time of year. I shopped with efficiency as I had already planned in my head what I was going to get and the quickest route to obtaining it all. After some indecision, I had chosen to buy Carol a small gift. It could be a thank you or a Christmas present depending on how we got on that afternoon. I was finished and returned to the bike within an hour and a half; my purchases small enough to fit into the luggage holder at the back of the Ducati. The ride home was trouble free, the tailbacks were for the cars heading into town rather than away from it.

I spent the next hour wrapping the gifts and writing cards. I am, like many men, completely useless with wrapping paper and sticky tape. The gifts looked like scrunched up pieces of paper by the time I was finished. My mother can always pick out my present to her under the tree before she reads the label.

Carol arrived at around 12:00. She was dressed casually with a hint of glamour in a shimmering white blouse over dark blue jeans. Her hair was gently curled, her make up was subtle and she looked sensational.

"You're looking a bit posh for someone here to help," I grinned at her.

"Oh, this old thing, just something the servants found at the back of my walk-in wardrobe," she replied in a posh English voice.

I laughed and led her into the living room.

"It's a bit dusty."

"That was the police, honest."

"Coffee?"

"Can I have a tea, please?"

"What do you take?"

"A spot of milk."

I brewed up in the kitchen and she came to talk to me. She stood leaning against the frame of the door, her shapely figure emphasised by her pose. I tried to keep my mind from wandering too far from the task at hand.

We chatted easily as if we had known each other for ages, a comfortable form of friendship was developing with none of the usual early awkwardness. When we had finished our drinks we began the clean up. Carol set to work with a duster and furniture polish while I finished putting the place back into some kind of order. I set my books, DVDs and CDs back into their correct shelves. Carol was amused at my rigorous filing system and teased me, asking me how long I had been OCD. After a couple of hours the house looked great and I suggested we go for a late lunch.

One of the advantages of living in the West End of Glasgow is that there is no shortage of places to eat. We went to La Riviera in Dumbarton Road, where the food is delicious and the prices are reasonable.

After we had ordered, Carol asked about the case.

I told her about Mrs Kilpatrick, Rory and what I had discovered about his death.

"It looks like this builder Maloney is up to his neck in it but I can't get near him."

"Oh, I seen something in the newspaper today. He is holding some Christmas party at his house, big do, with loads of important people, apparently."

"Is he now? I don't suppose you know where?"

"I'm sure it said that his house is near Mugdock Park, out by Milngavie."

"That gives me an idea. I think it might be worth gate-crashing, don't you?"

"Would that not be risky? If he's done what you think he's done."

"Maybe, but I don't think I will get past his bulldog of personal assistant at the firm, so this might be my best chance. I'm sorry we'll need to cut this a bit short."

She nodded a sad agreement.

"Look, I've had a great time today. I don't want you to think that I don't want to see you."

"I understand, this is important and you need to get it sorted out." I was pleased that she seemed to understand how crucial it was to me.

"If I can wrap this up, life will go back to normal, I promise."

"OK, OK, you've convinced me." She leaned over and squeezed my hand.

We spent the rest of the meal getting to know more about each other, sharing memories of school and university, laughing about her uncle and his little dogs.

When we were finished, we had a last coffee at the flat before she left for home. We shared a passionate and longing kiss before she left, leaving me with a warm glow at the prospect of spending more time with her.

When she had gone I phoned Barry and told him I would need my little job completed for tonight. He told me it was already finished and asked me what I was planning. I told him but he didn't seem too impressed.

*

I was ready to go to Maloney's around seven o'clock. I had phoned Barry and outlined the plan. He had managed to complete the little bit of work I had asked him to do, I stopped in at his house before the ride to Milngavie.

"Hi Barry," I said as he opened the door.

"Come in. It's ready to go."

"That's great."

"Are you sure you want to do this?"

"Absolutely. I've got nothing concrete to tie him to Rory's death, I need to get him talking."

"These are bad people, Craig. You might be next if you're not careful."

Everyone was keen to warn me of the dangers but I was determined to see it through, "I'm OK, I can look after myself. Now how does this work."

"You switch it on and it will start as soon as someone starts speaking."

"As easy as that? Thanks, Barry I owe you one."

"Please ring me when you're back at the flat." His unease at what I was doing was obvious.

"OK, will do. Thanks again." I left the flat and placed his workmanship in the bike's rear storage.

I turned on to Great Western Road and followed it as far as Anniesland Cross, then went right towards Bearsden and rode along the Switchback Road. At the roundabout, I took the Milngavie Road. After five miles I could see the lights of Maloney's house glinting through the small copse of trees that surrounded it. I manoeuvred the bike to the left, off the main road and headed down the driveway towards the lights.

The house was partially hidden until the last hundred yards or so. The drive was now covered in gravel; the house was to the right and there were several cars parked to the left. The whole area was well lit and I parked the bike between a black Bentley Continental and a silver Aston Martin DB9. I retrieved my spare helmet from the back of the bike, pressed a switch before placing my usual helmet in its place.

I had a good view of the house as I approached. The architecture was post-modern, an attractive combination of glass and white render. To the left of the main door was a circular glass tower, the curve at the front ran at a tangent to form the sharp line of the facade of the building. To the right of the door, the ground floor was glass, with the upper floor rendered in a brilliant white, the render broken up by a series of small square windows. I could hear the sound of party music coming from the ground floor and the number of people milling around inside meant that Mr. Maloney's party was well under way. The grounds of the house were extensively landscaped and I could see a small waterfall lit by coloured spotlights down at the far end of the building. There was a gap in the trees that would, during daylight, allow stunning views of the Campsie Hills but not enough to allow the poor plebs a sight of the house from the main road.

I rang the door bell and was greeted by an ape in a dinner suit. He was about 6 feet tall and half as much again wide, or so it seemed. The tuxedo jacket he wore was stretched to its limit by the breadth of his chest, his hands hung from it like two great legs of pork.

"Good evening, sir. May I see your invitation?" His voice, although deep, was surprisingly refined with a trace of an Irish lilt.

"I don't have an invitation. I need to see Mr. Maloney urgently."

"I'm afraid that's not possible. Mr Maloney is with his guests and does not want to be disturbed." He was courteous but his demeanour, stance and voice warned that he was not to be messed with.

"Can you tell him that my name is Craig Campbell and that I know what happened to Rory Kilpatrick?" If he had been warned about me his reactions did not betray it.

"I will try, sir, but you will have to leave if he doesn't wish to talk to you. Would you care to wait in the reception room?"

"That would be great, thank you."

He showed me into a room that formed the ground floor of the tower I had seen from outside. I watched the immense breadth of his back as he lumbered off to find his master like an obedient bulldog.

The single circular wall, which stretched two thirds of the way round the room, was tastefully decorated with inoffensive magnolia paint, abstract art placed to add some colour and a couple of simple sofas. The beautifully finished real oak floor flowed from the hall into this room, a simple statement of taste and elegance. There was a splash of Christmas, red and white flowers, professionally arranged, in a vase on a rectangular sideboard behind one of the sofas. There was also a coffee table made from what looked like teak with a glass top. I stood inside the door rather than taking a seat. Although I wouldn't have minded if any of the dirt from my leathers had spoiled the furniture.

I waited a couple of minutes before King Kong reappeared, "Mr. Maloney will see you in his office, sir. If you would care to follow me."

I did as I was told and he led me to a spectacular spiral staircase, beautifully crafted in the same rich oak as the floor. From the top I could see down from a gallery space into the main living area. A large number of people wandered around, dressed in their party finery. One or two danced and a few were lined up along a table with food and drink artfully arranged on it. The end of the table featured a reindeer, sculpted with exquisite skill from a block of ice. My chunky pal showed me to a heavy curved door that was directly above the reception room.

"Thanks, Mark. Can you wait a moment?" Maloney stood behind a substantial desk, dressed in an expensive tuxedo with a white shirt and bow tie. He was short, around five feet, six inches, fit looking for his age but his eyes betrayed his years. He was balding, what hair he had was turning grey from a pale red base. He had the air of a man in control of himself and others; a man who was used to getting things done the way he wanted them.

"Ah, Mr Campbell, I've heard a lot about you. You've been creating quite a stir." There was no trace of the Gorbals in his accent, it was the posh tone that Glaswegians referred to as Kelvinside, in Edinburgh, it was Morningside. It is Scottish but the vowels are more rounded, the emphasis subtly different from how the majority of Scots phrase a sentence. An attempt to blend in with his upper class friends, no doubt.

"I try my best. Sorry, I'm a little under dressed." I replied with an assuredness that I hardly felt.

His smile was strained and insincere, with his skin moisturised to a subtle sheen, he looked like an eighties game show host.

"Before we start our little chat, can I just check that you have no recording equipment on your person. I don't want anything I say to be taken out of context, that would be a bit embarrassing and a little inconvenient. Mark, would you do the honours?"

I placed my helmet on a glass table that was in front of low, black leather chairs. Mark patted me down and made me open my leathers before lifting my shirt.

"Ooh saucy, is this how you get your kicks, Mark?" The guard ignored me and completed his search with the efficiency of a customs officer.

"Thank you for your co-operation Mr Campbell, a man in my position can't be too careful. Thanks, Mark, that'll be all for now."

Mark left us alone in the stunning office. Unlike the room below, this was almost completely glass, with views through the trees to a small loch behind the house, down the drive and off to the Campsies at the front. Everything lit tastefully to show it off to its best advantage.

"So, Craig, can I call you Craig?"

"Why not, we're all friends here." I tried to match his tone, I had read somewhere that it helped to build rapport.

"Please take a seat." He indicated one of the low chairs and he sat opposite me. I settled into the comfortable leather of the chair.

"How can I help you?

Time to stop the dance, "I think you know why I'm here or you wouldn't have agreed to see me."

"The unfortunate Rory Kilpatrick, such a tragic accident." His words dripped with the insincerity of an American TV evangelist.

"Cut the bull, I'm not really in the mood for games." His arrogance had already begun to get under my skin.

"I'm not sure what you mean."

"I know that Rory was making trouble for you and that the night before he died, your pal Callaghan warned you that Rory was about to make his concerns official."

He smiled, "Ah, poor Joe. He always was one for panicking and getting stressed by the least wee thing. I'm sure that's what led to his stroke."

"Rory had worked out that you winning the tender for the schools wasn't based on the quality of the tender but on the help you received from inside the council." I watched him for some reaction but his face remained emotionless.

"I had a little help, but that's just the way the world works. You scratch my back I'll scratch yours. It's not what you know blah, blah, blah." He waved his hand in a dismissive gesture.

"It turned into some very severe scratches. Deep scratches that will get you noticed."

"I know you've got no evidence that would stand up in court and I'm pretty sure Joe won't talk to the police anytime soon. If you had anything it would be the fraud squad I was talking to not a cheap imitation one man band."

"How do you know what I've got?'

"Well, you see, after Mr Kilpatrick's unfortunate accident, I had some people check out his flat, his computer at work and even his girlfriend's flat." He said as if he was explaining something to a child.

"Like you checked out my office and home?"

He looked genuinely surprised. "No, I don't know anything about that. As I say I knew there was nothing for you to find."

"You're lying. You got one of your goons to ransack my place and they killed an old woman in the process." Despite knowing that I had to try and stay in control, I could feel a smouldering rage begin to flame.

"I'm afraid I don't know what you're talking about. Maybe it was an accident but it definitely had nothing to do with me.' He seemed sincere and I had my first doubt.

"There's a lot of accidents about. What about Swanson?"

"Well, if it'll put you out of your misery, I'll tell you the whole story. Joe recruited one or two in the office to help him with my little project, I don't know all the details. Swanson was one of them as Joe knew that he was more pliable than some of the staff he had under him. He had gambling debts that would have shocked some Premiership Footballers."

He smiled at his own weak joke. His smugness was getting on my nerves. I had hoped to rattle him considerably more than I had achieved so far.

"It was all going to plan until Mr. Kilpatrick stuck his nose into my business. I own a security firm, Craig, one of my profitable enterprises. There are some people there you wouldn't like to cross." It was the first real emotion, a hint of threat behind his words,

"They've been useful in helping to alleviate some minor problems I've had down through the years. I asked them to take care of the obstacle to the successful completion of my tender contract. By the following night my troubles had disappeared, just like magic. Then a couple of months later Swanson started to make noises about blackmailing Joe and I. Another call and another problem was solved." His voice was almost monotone, devoid of any emotion other than a trace of pride at a job well done. "So you see how the problem was dealt with had nothing to do with me, I just asked my guys to look after it for me, it's not my fault if they got a little bit over-enthusiastic."

"Why? You were already a wealthy man, God, you might have won the contract anyway."

"Craig, you can't be sure of anything in this life, so sometimes you have to eliminate the element of chance. I've never been a gambler. I don't leave anything to the fates if I can avoid it. You ask why? Simple, money. I knew the housing market was about to die a rapid death and I have been proved right with everything that has happened since. I needed a secure source of income and God bless them the government laid it on a big tempting plate for me. You can't imagine how much more secure my company's future was when we won that contract. It's not just for me, think of the jobs it guaranteed." It was the kind of nonsense that made me want pick up the helmet and beat him senseless.

"So what about the Labour Party, the charity work? Is it all just a big sham?"

"Oh the Labour Party was genuine to start with but Thatcher changed everything, including the Labour Party. Socialism is such a dirty word these days, the free market reigns supreme. Look at who the major contributors are to either of the main parties and there isn't a lot of difference between them. Policies are much the same, the Tories would have allowed the banks to mess things up just the way the Labour Party did, they're indivisible. PPP is just the latest way to take taxpayers money and put it into the pockets of people like myself. The Entrepreneurs. All the government is these days is a collection agency for their contractors.' He laughed in slightly creepy way.

"Thatcher started it when she sold off everything. A new era of choice and better service was what they said in public but the reality quickly hit home and we now have publicly funded millionaires. Brilliant. I wish I had got in at the start but I was a little slow to realise the potential and petty moral objections blocked my path to the real money. I've caught up now and I'm just taking my turn at milking the public cash cow. There is only one game in town now and that's to get as rich as you can. Without money you're nothing."

I felt like punching him, the rant was the empty sound of a self-obsessed man, a man whose only worth was in what he owned and how much money he had. Any trace of humanity was buried under a bank vault.

"And all of that makes it OK to kill people."

"There are always casualties, Craig. Iraq was an excuse to open up a new market for British and American companies, Afghanistan is about fuel and pipelines. Every tragedy is an opportunity for the people who want to make something of themselves. I've done nothing wrong compared with the bigger fish. I just got someone to take care of a couple of minor problems."

I wondered whether he was deranged, he seemed to have a sociopath's emotionless persona. Did he really not know the difference between right and wrong or was it an act, designed to disgust me? If so, he had definitely succeeded.

"You're very sure of yourself aren't you?"

"Why shouldn't I be? I'm the owner and Chief Executive of a multimillion pound business. The law, like taxes, is for the little people, like yourself. People like me get awards from the Queen and plaudits from politicians."

"You go on thinking that. I'm sure the little people who populate the ranks of the police force will take great pleasure in pulling your empire down around your ears."

There was a knock on the door and a bleached blonde woman walked in.

"Come in my dear. Craig, this is my wife, Charlotte."

She turned to me "Hello, I'm sorry to disturb you dear but we're about to do the presents." She had the look of the ageing wife of a footballer, all peroxide hair, expensive jewellery and permanent tan. She was at least fifteen years younger than her husband.

"I'll be there in a minute, darling."

"Nice meeting you, sorry for disturbing you," she said as she left.

"That's fine, I think we're finished.

"Are you going so soon? I was enjoying our little chat but I suppose I must get back to my guests."

When his wife was out of earshot I said, "Do they know the amoral leech you really are?"

"Now, Craig no need to be like that." He walked to the desk and pressed a button. Moments later Mark appeared at the door. "Mr Campbell, is leaving us now, Mark. Show him out would you?"

I turned to face Maloney before I left, "I look forward to the day they throw you in Barlinnie."

"I don't think you need to worry about that Mr. Campbell, I won't be going anywhere, but thank you for your concern." He smiled again but the coldness of his eyes remained. I walked out, my blood roaring in my ears as I struggled for control.

The anger I felt was tempered by the fact that I had managed to get the details I needed to let the police deal with him. I placed my spare helmet back in my luggage box, safe in the knowledge that the recorder Barry had fitted into it would have enough information to convict Maloney of corruption and hopefully Rory's murder. I knew that I would need to find who else was involved, I owed it to Mrs. Capaldi.

I squeezed into my other helmet and pushed the starter on the bike. I rode down the drive and then turned right to head back to Glasgow. After a minute or two I noticed a set of headlights behind but I thought nothing of it until the car suddenly pulled alongside me and started to ease towards me, narrowing the road in front of me. I hammered hard on the bike's horn but the car kept coming. I braked heavily and let the back of the bike swing round. It began to slide away from me but the wheels gripped in time bringing me to a stand still. I was facing away from Glasgow, I looked over my shoulder, the car had now braked and was turning back towards me. I could see the blue propeller logo of a BMW heading in my direction.

I accelerated with all the bike could give me, knowing that it would out run any car over a short distance but on a long straight the car could chase me down. I knew enough of these roads to calculate any number of alternative routes to Glasgow. I looked down at the speedometer, the needle was pointing at 80 MPH but a quick check of my mirrors and I could see the lights were growing larger again.

Up ahead were two sharp bends on a stretch of road that was downhill leading to the village of Strathblane. I dare not go any faster as I was approaching the first corner. I changed down into third gear and down again into second before sweeping to my right leaning over the lane for oncoming traffic like a racer as I tried to maintain enough grip on a road that had been gritted against the snow and ice. I had to straighten up very quickly as there was a car coming in the opposite direction; the horn blared angrily at me. I heard the brakes of the car behind me screech like a wounded fox as the driver desperately tried to slow down enough to take the bend. Before I could look back to see what had happened I was on to the second turn, this time it was necessary to swing the bike over to the left as quickly and as hard as I could to make the hairpin curve. The bike began to skid and I had a brief flashback of my accident. The wide tyres suddenly found some traction and I moved in the direction I needed to go. I was never so glad to have had relatively new tyres.

The road then took a gentler turn to the right before I entered the village of Strathblane itself. I slowed the bike and looked behind me, the car was not in sight and I had to decide where to go. I remembered there was a road at the other end of the small village that was used by hill walkers to begin a traipse over the Campsies. Ignoring the possibility of speed cameras, I rode as fast as I dared go to get to the road before the car spotted me. I reached Campsie Dene Road and went up it about 100 yards before stopping and killing my lights. I could see the main road from my vantage point and watched as the BMW sped past the turn off and headed out towards Drumgoyne and Killearn.

I knew it wouldn't take him long to realise that he was going the wrong way and that he would turn back. I rode the bike back down the hill and back to the main road. Instead of going back the way I had come in, I turned left on the road to Lennoxtown and Milton of Campsie. Once out of Strathblane, I rode the Ducati hard as I needed to put as much distance between me and the BMW as I could. I had nearly reached Lennoxtown when a pair of headlights appeared in my mirrors again. Once in the village, I decided the only way to rid myself of them was on a twisty road that would give the bike the advantage. I turned on to the B822, Crow Road as it is called; it briefly crossed my mind that going the crow road was an old Scots expression for death. In the pitch black it is a dangerous road, leading into the hills, it is a road of steep inclines and lots of tricky corners. There was a thin sheen of ice and snow on the ungritted road. Adhesion was difficult but I knew that the rear wheel drive of the BMW would also struggle. I hoped to have an advantage as I knew the road well. The Campsies are a great place to take the bike for a run in the brightness of the summer sun but I was gambling that my knowledge would hold up on a moonless winter's night.

The bike was responsive to my every movement, accelerating when I could, braking hard when I needed to whilst being aware of the road conditions, swinging from left to right and back again. The lights began to drift further behind me as the less nimble four wheels failed to cope with the suppleness of the Ducati's two. At Craigton, I turned right on to the B818, more twists and turns left the car far behind me and by the time I passed the Carron Valley reservoir, I only glimpsed the headlights occasionally. I reached Carron Bridge a good two or three miles ahead of the BMW and turned into the Tak-ma-doon Road that brought me out in Kilsyth.

*

The rest of the journey back to Glasgow, through Kirkintilloch and Bishopbriggs was uneventful. I arrived back in Chancellor Street around ten o'clock. I carried both helmets with me into the flat. As promised, I rang Barry and told him what had happened, before I could stop him he had truncated the phone call and was on his way over.

He arrived with Li about ten minutes later, a mixture of anxiety and anger could be seen on both their faces.

"What the hell were you thinking?" Li was the first to give me a hard time.

"I needed to get something that would prove what I suspected. I needed to go to the source."

Barry was next to tear into me, "I told you that you were messing with some real nasty people, Craig. What would have happened if that car had caught you? You would have just been another accident statistic."

"I know that but it was worth it, check this out." I handed him the helmet and he extracted the recorder from the lining and disconnected it from the miniature microphone he had fitted into the front. He pressed the play button and the whole conversation with Maloney played to their silent astonishment.

"He's nuts" Li said.

"Totally gaga," Barry agreed.

"He doesn't really say that he ordered Rory's or Barry's death, just that he asked the security guys to take care of it," Li observed.

"I know, a good lawyer would probably do enough to raise reasonable doubt in the minds of a jury. The stuff about the corruption will put him away for a while, particularly with documentation that Rory collected to confirm it."

"So that's it then you can turn it over to the police?" Barry asked.

"Not quite. I need to find who's responsible for Mrs. Capaldi's death and that is definitely personal."

"Christ, Craig, you're as nuts as Maloney. Haven't you had enough of people trying to kill you?" Li was forcible in his opinion.

"I owe it to Mrs. C. Whoever it is, they caused the death of a decent woman who deserved better than to die like that. I need to be the one that puts him away."

"But you can't do that without the police."

"I don't want the police involved until I've finished with him."

Barry drew a long sigh before he said, "Bonkers, absolutely bonkers. What are you planning?"

"I'm not sure yet but I need to try and get something tomorrow. Then I'll hand Callaghan, Maloney and all their cohorts to DC Cooper and DCI Munro."

"You've lost your mind, this isn't some story of the old west where the gunslinger rounds up the villains and tosses them to the Sheriff. You're not Clint Eastwood, this is real life, your life. You've done enough."

I was annoyed at them, I couldn't work out why they didn't understand how I felt, that I needed to resolve this and maybe that I needed to ease my own conscience. If I hadn't been involved, Mrs. Capaldi would still be here. I rationalised that there was only one way to do something for her and that was to catch her killer.

"I need to do this, take my word for it. Barry can you take a copy of the recording and be ready to deliver it to the police tomorrow?"

"Craig.."

"Please, just do it. I don't want to hear any more."

"OK," he replied with reluctance.

I laid out my plan for the following day so they knew where I was going and what I was going to do.

"If there are any changes, I'll let you know."

"Fine, but I still think you're nuts," Li's anger was barely disguised in his tone.

They said their farewells and left me to my own thoughts. I hoped the next day would bring an to end this and I was looking forward to putting it all behind me.

Chapter Twelve

At 9:30, on a freezing Sunday morning, I found myself sitting in a coffee shop in Bothwell Street, opposite the HQ of Secure New Future. During a restless night, I had devised a plan to speak to someone in the security firm who could maybe shed some light on exactly what happened to Rory. I wasn't sure if anyone would be about their offices on a Sunday but I hoped that being the weekend before Christmas would mean that there was plenty of staff on duty at shops across the city.

The owner of the coffee shop almost seemed shocked to see me as I walked in within seconds of her opening the doors of her small establishment. She was in her fifties, dressed in a rainbow of colours that made her look vaguely like an ageing hippy. She wore a pair of glasses around her neck on a lanyard and brought them up to her face when she operated the electronic till. She didn't offer much conversation, which suited me fine.

I ordered a large cappuccino and took a seat at the window where I had a good view of the entrance to the office. I watched while snow drifted down, people rushing past in a hurry to be out of the arctic conditions. It was an hour before anyone joined me in the warmth and a further two cups of decaffeinated coffee before I saw anyone go into the Secure New Future building. A young woman unlocked the door and disappeared into the dark of the entrance. At least I knew there would be some activity. I wasn't convinced that she would be much help, so I decided to wait a bit longer.

My patience was rewarded at 11:45 when Mark, the polite doorman for the previous night, appeared from the passenger seat of a black BMW 3 series and walked into the offices. The car drove away. I finished my coffee and wrapped myself in my leathers. I crossed the street and stood in a doorway two down from where my quarry had gone.

Despite being wrapped in three layers of clothing, the wind found its way into a variety of crevices in my body. I had been standing for about forty five minutes when Mark walked past me heading for Hope Street. I fell in behind him and followed him for a short time. Halfway up the hill I called his name. He turned and there was a brief moment before he recognised me.

"Mr. Campbell, isn't it?"

I was struck once again by the incongruity of the quietly spoken Irish lilt coming from such a substantial figure.

"Mark, I wonder if I could talk to you."

He smiled and offered politely, "I'm not sure I would have anything to say that would be of any interest to you."

"I'm sure you're a very interesting guy. Let me buy you lunch and we can have a chat."

"There's nothing I will say that will help you, if you're after my employer." Although his words retained the courteous theme, there was a element of steel in his tone that fired a gentle first warning.

"Your boss is in trouble no matter what you say, but you might be able to stop him going to jail for murder."

"Murder, ha. You're kidding, right?"

"Well that depends on what you can tell me."

I could see him weighing his thoughts before he decided. "OK, I'll give you half an hour."

We walked a short distance up Hope Street to a small Italian restaurant. We were shown to a table, I ordered a tuna sandwich with some sparkling mineral water, while Mark requested some minestrone soup. When the waitress had finished delivering the order, I began my pitch between bites of the focaccia bread.

"How long have you worked for Mr Maloney?"

"About three years."

"What did you do before that?"

"I was a soldier."

His answers and demeanour suggested someone who used as few words as possible.

"What do you know about Rory Kilpatrick's death?"

"An awful accident wasn't it?"

"I'm sure that you know a bit more than that. Your boss suggested that you and some of your colleagues took care of a little problem for him, in fact two problems, if you include Brian Swanson."

"I didn't kill either of them, in fact no one in our organisation did, if that's what you're suggesting."

"You're sure of that?"

He bobbed a defiant positive nod. "Absolutely, everyone involved at this level are disciplined soldiers, they follow orders."

"What were the orders?"

"We were to give Kilpatrick a warning to back off, that's it."

"Tell me what happened the night Rory died."

"I got a call from Mr. Maloney around lunch time. He told me that he needed Kilpatrick to be encouraged not to make any further reports or investigations into the bidding process. Joe Callaghan would get someone to call from the party to tell me when Kilpatrick left, myself and a colleague were to pick him up as he left. Around eight I got a call from Davie Stone."

"Stone?"

The surprise was clearly written over my face. "Yes, didn't you know that he was involved. He was one of Callaghan's boys on the inside."

"What happened after you got the call?"

"Stone had apparently told Rory that he had some information for him, that Stone had decided to get out because he thought that what was going on was wrong. He told Rory to meet him outside. He must be some actor because Kilpatrick believed him. He walked out the hotel and was heading along Argyle Street. I grabbed him with the help of a colleague and we took him into an alley. We threatened him and his girlfriend for a while and then roughed him up a bit. My mate called for a car, the plan was to leave him in another part of town, steal his wallet and make it look like a mugging."

"So what changed?"

"Just as the car arrived, Stone appeared. He said he would take care of it. We bundled Kilpatrick into the car, handed Stone the keys and left him to it."

I struggled to know what to say, "What state was Rory in?"

"We had roughed him up but he would have recovered," he replied as if beating someone up was like a routine matter.

"Had he been drinking?"

"Not that I could tell."

"Was he ready to forget about the tender stuff?"

"We're professionals, Mr Campbell. He got the message." Pride at a job well done turned the edge of his mouth up in an involuntary smile.

I felt stunned. Rory wasn't the only one who had been taken in by Stone's acting.

"So why doesn't Maloney know this?"

"Let's just say that Mr Maloney isn't interested in the details of anything we do for him. It's better that way. He thinks we dealt with it in a way that keeps him just a little scared of us. It means he doesn't hold all the aces."

"What about Swanson?"

"Genuinely an accident as far as I know. We never got a chance to talk to him. He was up to his eyes in debt, maybe he took the easy way out. Maybe Mr. Stone did a bit of freelancing again, I don't know."

"And you just let Maloney think that was something else you took care of?"

"Yes. I respect Mr Maloney and I like him respecting me, it keeps me in work."

There was a strange dispassionate quality to him that was disconcerting. Violence was a job to him, inflicting injury was nothing personal, there was no anger, no zeal, it was purely a business transaction.

"If I give this story to police what would you do?"

"Mr. Maloney's lawyers would advise them that they have no proof and I would go back to work."

"You know that Maloney will be going to jail for fraud, you might not have a job to go back to."

"Court rooms are funny things, lawyers make mistakes, a jury can make strange decisions, judges can interpret the law in unusual ways. Nothing is certain."

I wondered if he was hinting that Maloney wasn't above coercion or bribery of the judicial system. I wouldn't have put it past him based on his rant of the previous night.

"Was it one of your colleagues that tried to give me and my bike an introduction to a tree last night?"

"Sorry?"

"Someone tried to run me off the road when I left the party last night."

"Nothing to do with us." His denial was adamant and I believed he was telling the truth.

"What about Rory and his mother, do you feel anything for them?"

"I'm sorry that he's dead but it had nothing to do with me."

"OK. My sandwich has lost its flavour, there's a horrible taste in my mouth. I'll pay the bill and leave you to your soup."

I signalled the waitress, paid the bill and got up to leave. As he reached the door, Mark called out to me,"Mr Campbell"

I turned.

"Thanks for lunch."

I was tempted to slam the door but I reined in my frustration and stepped out without acknowledging him.

*

The new information I had about Stone had shocked me but the more I thought about it the more I realised that all of his help had been directing me to Derek Norman. It was all a smoke screen, designed to point me at someone that had no connection to the crime and consequently there would never have been any evidence to get the case to court.

I rode back to the flat and decided to challenge Stone, there was now too much to point to him and I hoped that I could force a confession out of him. Before I could call him my mobile rang. The caller ID told me it was Stone.

"Hello" I tried to keep the excitement out of my voice.

"Hi, it's Davie Stone. I've got some information for you."

"I was just about to ring you, go on then."

"No, no I need to see you. I don't want to talk about it over the phone."

"OK, I'll come to your place."

"No, definitely not. My mother's not feeling too good. There's a place off Dalmarnock Road, Bartholomew Street, no one will see us." There was a nervous crackle in his voice.

"Are you all right, Davie?"

"Look, I don't want anybody seeing me talking to you, that's all."

I decided to play along, "Is it Maloney, has he said something?"

"Do you want this information or not?" he asked abruptly.

"Fine. I'll come." He gave me directions and we arranged to meet at three o'clock.

After the chill of the morning, I changed into warmer clothing as the snow continued to fall across the city. The roads were treacherous for two wheels, I still had the keys to Li's car and decided it was the safer option.

The journey to Dalmarnock Road was straightforward, if slow due to the Christmas shopping traffic and the effect of the weather. It took me about ten minutes to find Bartholomew Street, I had missed the turn and had to drive around before locating it. I parked a couple of streets away and walked through the sizable white flakes to the building. I arrived at about two forty-five which was a little later than I had planned but it still gave me time to have a look around. While I walked back to the address, I sent Barry and Li a text to let them know that the plan had changed and where I was going.

The warehouse was obviously designed to cater for large lorries, there was a considerable amount of space in front of the loading bay. The building itself was constructed of a charcoal grey brick, the doors on the loading bay were blue although the paint was peeling. To the left there was a room that looked like it used to house offices. Vandals had broken the windows, the door had been kicked open and now sat a precarious angle. The whole structure was enclosed by a high wall, constructed from the same brick as the building. Large metal, white gates lay open, probably rusted into immobility. The street was deserted and there were no houses overlooking the property. There was definitely no chance of anyone watching us without us knowing.

I walked back to where the car was parked and waited until five to three before driving round to the warehouse. There was an old blue BMW parked close to the loading bay, but there was no sign of the driver. I drew up behind the Beemer and took another quick look around before I got out of the car. A prickle of suspicion engulfed me as I looked at the propeller logo. As I walked towards the office, the snow danced around me, waltzing to a mournful tune whistled by the wind.

"Campbell."

I turned to see Stone walk out from a sheltered area of the loading bay. I walked to the steps that would take me up to the level that the lorries would have picked up their freight. Stone stayed in the shadows but what I could see of him was pale, looking overweight and sweating profusely. A tingle of anxiety played at the edge of my consciousness.

"Davie. Are you OK?"

"I'll be fine, when we're finished here." His voice quivered and my unease climbed a bit further up the scale towards fear.

"You've got some information for me?"

"Very funny, Campbell. You're a fucking comedian."

"Davie, you phoned me, remember?"

"I thought I would save you the trouble of tracking me down."

"Tracking you down? What are you talking about?" The only way I could try and keep him off guard was to play it dumb, to let him think I knew nothing.

"You were at Maloney's last night, I know, I followed you. Don't think I don't know what he told you." His voice was edgy.

"He told me he was up to his neck in corruption and it'll probably put him in jail."

"Aye, well I'll not be joining him."

I sighed. "He didn't know you were involved but someone else did."

"I knew it. Who was it that Bruce bitch?" He stayed in the shadows but stepped towards me and I raised to hands to placate him.

"No. Someone who knew what went on that night, someone who was there."

"Aw, shit."

"Maloney only told me that Callaghan had recruited some people in the office. Apart from Swanson, he said he didn't know any names."

"Well that was a lie but it doesn't matter, you know now.

Here was me thinking you had it all worked out. I even tried to see what evidence you had, too."

"I have it worked out but not because of Maloney."

As I spoke a dreadful truth suddenly alighted on me. "You killed Mrs. Capaldi."

"Who?" he looked shocked.

"Mrs. Lucia Capaldi. My neighbour. You remember her, the seventy five year-old woman that you pushed down the stairs in my tenement close. The lady whose skull was fractured, the lady who died as a result of her injuries, the lady that you, Brian Stone, murdered."

"It was an accident. What was the stupid old bitch doing, sticking her nose in anyway. I just brushed her on the stair and she fell." His face seemed to carry some remorse, I wondered if Mrs. Capaldi made him think of his own mother.

"A double murderer. So what was it Davie, the money. Did Maloney offer you a fortune?" I pressed him firmly for answers despite the fact that he still seemed to be on edge.

"What? Are you wanting, a cut? You've had it, 'cause I've got nothing to give you."

"What, spent it all already?"

"No. Let's say it's tied up in property."

"Oh, same as Joe. Where's your bargain residence, then?"

"Marbella, if you must know."

"Very nice, you must be Mr. Maloney's special friend. But I suppose there's no one else left to do his bidding, now that Callaghan's disabled and Swanson's dead." The anger showed in my voice for the first time.

His voice also began to rise, but his was an amplified panic, "It's got nothing to do with me."

"What do you mean it's got nothing to do with you? You murdered Rory, you drove him to that railway line, you poured drink into him and then left him on that line to die. You knew what you were doing, what I don't understand is why."

He stepped out of the shadow, drawing a large kitchen knife from inside his coat.

"I can't go to jail, I can't leave mother, she needs me." He waved the knife in my direction. "You, you're a liar, you've got no proof, this is a big bluff to make me scared."

In response I lowered my tone and slowed my speech slightly in an effort to sound reassuring, "Put the knife down, Davie. My friends know I'm here, they will call the police with all the details if I don't go back."

"More fuckin' lies,' he screamed and moved closer to me.

"I'm not lying, it's the truth." I was struggling to keep the terror I felt out of my voice, I realised that Stone was unstable and liable to do anything.

"Who are you to judge me, you don't know what it's been like? I've looked after my mother for years, I wanted something better for both of us and Maloney gave me the chance. What harm was I doing? Kilpatrick was an arse-hole, I begged him to keep quiet. I told him that he could get something as well but he had to be Peter fucking Perfect. Joe made me set him up that night, I thought they were going to rough him up a bit but then I decided I had to be sure. If I could get rid of him that would make sure he never talked to anyone. I followed Maloney's guys and I heard them call for the car. I presumed they wouldn't use one of their own cars so I asked to take him. When I got away from them, I drove to a deserted car park, he was still groggy from the beating. I had a hip-flask filled with whisky and I came up with the plan to get rid of him. Make him look like a drunk, a wee ironic touch that as he was always "holier than thou" about the dangers of alcohol. I poured the whisky into him and then I got the tyre wrench out of the car and hit him on the head with it. After that I drove about for ages thinking how to get rid of him. Then the railway idea struck me, a perfect way to get rid of the evidence, make it look like an accident. I found a gap in the fence, dragged him on to a line that was obviously in use and left him there. I drove the car to some wasteland and torched it." Tears welled up in his eyes but the knife stayed firmly pointed at me.

"What about Swanson?"

"That was nothing to do with me, that was between Maloney and Callaghan. Swanson told me he was going to try and sweat Maloney for more cash, he was convinced he was on a winner. I told him he was stupid but he was in hock to some bookie and needed the cash so there was no dissuading him. It was his own fault."

The knife was lowered a little as he spoke.

"Davie, put the knife down and this can all end here." I'm sure my voice was trembling as a combination of cold and dread affected me physically.

He shouted again. "Don't tell me what to do, I'm sick of people ordering me around. My mother, Callaghan,

Maloney; everybody knows what's best for me. I'm not doing it any more, so you shut the fuck up or I'll shut you up permanently." He raised the knife again and moved closer to me. I backed off a little further but I was getting close to the edge of the loading bay.

"Davie, for Christ's sake, what are you doing? You can't get away with this, Maloney and his cronies will drop you at the first chance to save their own skins."

"Fuckin' shut it." He lunged, the knife pointing at my heart. I tried to divert it with my left hand as I moved to the right; the knife cut through the sleeve of my jacket and I felt a stinging, burning pain across my arm. My sleeve turned a dark crimson red, the blood seeping through the layers of my clothes instantly. He lost his balance and was in danger of falling but somehow stopped himself before he tumbled off the loading bay. He turned to face me again, his expression full of rage.

"This isn't how this should end. My mates know where I am, they will tell the police and you won't be seeing your mother except in the visitor room at Barlinnie."

"Shut it, shut it, you're a fuckin' liar."

He waved the knife at me again, as if brandishing a sword. I knew that the only way I could end this was to take the initiative. As he began to move towards me again, I moved my balance to the right and used my left foot to kick out at his right hand and the knife it held. He moved surprisingly quickly and edged the weapon out of my reach. With my leg vulnerable he stabbed at my thigh, placing a lengthy nick above my knee. I backed off again, this time

I feinted as if I was going to use the same kick again but instead brought my right foot around into his chest. This time I connected perfectly and he stumbled back, I could see him heading towards the stairs, I reached to stop him falling but I was too late. He fell down the steps and landed on top of the knife.

I rushed down after him, the knife had plunged into his stomach. He lay there holding the wound, trying to stem the flow of blood.

"Shit. Hold on Davie, hold on." I took off my own blood stained jacket, I rolled it into a ball and pressed it against the wound.

The colour was draining from his face, "I guess it does end here."

"Don't be stupid, just stay with me."

"Tell my ma that I'm sorry. I just wanted a better life for her." Tears began to trickle down his pallid face leaving the same trails I had seen on the boy in the Western Infirmary. "Tell the old lady's family that I'm sorry about their mother, I didn't mean to hurt her. I'm sorry for everything. " He struggled for a breath and winced in pain. He began to sweat and I could see the life ebbing away from him.

"Come on, Stone, don't give up."

His eyes glazed over, the spark of life being extinguished and there was nothing I could do about it. His head lolled to the right and his final breath escaped his lips. I laid him gently down on the ground and tried to stand up. I felt dizzy and had to sit down again, I looked at my chest and realised that the knife had slashed across my left pectoral muscle and there was a significant amount of blood across my shirt and jacket. I struggled to concentrate as I tried to get my mobile phone out of my pocket. After what seemed an age I managed to retrieve it and dial the stored number for DC Cooper.

"Hello, Partick CID, Detective Constable Cooper, speaking"

"DC Cooper it's me, Craig Campbell."

"Craig, are you OK?"

"Not really, I'm at an old warehouse in Bartholomew Street in Dalmarnock. Can you get here as soon as you can?"

"What's up?'

"I'm with the guy that killed Mrs. Capaldi." I paused as I tried to focus on what I was going to say. "He killed Rory Kilpatrick too and if you send someone around to my mate Barry Fraser he'll give you the rest of the evidence. Oh and send an ambulance." I dropped the phone as the snow settled on my face and I slumped into a faint.

Epilogue

I awoke in Glasgow's Royal Infirmary, a series of bandages swathed around my chest, thigh and arm. A drip was attached to my right arm and there were some machines at the side of my bed. A young police officer was stationed at the end of my bed. He hadn't noticed me opening my eyes and he looked about as bored as anyone could.

"Hello," I croaked. My mouth and throat were dry. The noise seemed to startle the youthful cop and he jumped.

"Oh, Mr. Campbell. I'll get the nurse."

He disappeared and came back with a thickset, middle-aged nurse. He left me to her tender care and she looked at me with almost maternal concern. "Hello, I'm Mary-Ann. How are you?"

"Relieved."

"You were a lucky boy, ten minutes more and the paramedics would have been picking up a corpse. Do you need any painkillers?"

I did but I was happy just to be alive and pain was the confirmation of that so I said, "I'm all right at the moment, thanks. How long have I been out?"

"Just under 2 days. The police will want to speak to you, if you're not up to it, let me know. I'll keep them away." She smiled as if she would relish being my rottweiler.

"No, I'll see them."

"OK, I'll tell the PC." She checked some of the machines that were connected to various parts of my body and left me alone. My eyes grew heavy and I drifted off to sleep.

The next time I opened my eyes, it was DCI Munro that was my guardian angel.

"You're not very good at taking a warning, are you?"

"It's a character flaw, ask my mother, she'll tell you." I sounded like I had been gargling with gravel.

"Do you want some water?"

"Yes, please."

He poured a glass of water and handed it to me. With a little difficulty, I manoeuvred the plastic container to my lips. The cool liquid was as welcome as nectar.

"You took a terrible risk, doing what you did. What happened at the warehouse?"

"He was unstable, came at me with the knife, I kicked out to defend myself and he fell down the steps on to the knife. There was nothing I could do."

"Why didn't you tell us, let us deal with it?"

"I owed it to Mrs. Kilpatrick and particularly Mrs. Capaldi."

He shook his head, "I understand but I can't say I agree with your methods. You could have easily been lying in the mortuary."

"I know and believe me I'm very pleased not to be. Did you get Maloney?"

"He's been talking to the fraud squad. We've been quizzing his security guard pals and they're the best singers since Pavarotti. They claim that Maloney ordered a beating, but that they didn't kill anyone. He, of course, denies it. We're working on it but the documentation Rory gathered will definitely put him away for a while. People aren't particularly sympathetic to the greedy rich at the moment."

"What about Callaghan?"

"He's looking at jail time, I'm afraid."

"I feel sorry for his wife, she's had a hellish time of it."

"There's nothing we can do, Callaghan's almost as guilty Maloney."

"Have you spoken to Mrs. Kilpatrick or Isabel?"

"We've spoken to Mrs. Kilpatrick. She's very grateful for everything you've done." It was exactly what I needed to hear.

"It'll only be done when Maloney gets convicted. He might not have ordered Rory's death but he was definitely indirectly responsible." The pain and exhaustion overwhelmed me again. DCI Munro sensed it and left me to sleep again.

The next two days were filled with periods of sleep and recuperation, punctuated by a stream of visitors.

Li, Barry and Paul arrived for visiting on the first afternoon, bringing my mum who had travelled down from Arbroath. There was the usual banter from the guys, tempered with the concern of my mother for me; she was particularly quiet, not her usual self at all.

Isabel and Mrs. Kilpatrick appeared at the first evening visiting time. They arrived together and there seemed to be a degree of warmth between them that made me feel a little better.

"Mr. Campbell, we're so grateful for everything you've done. I never thought anyone would take me seriously enough to get an answer but I'm so glad you did." Mrs. Kilpatrick had tears in her eyes as she pressed my hand in gratitude. Despite those tears I could see that a weight had been lifted from her, a small measure of the stress brought on by Rory's death had dissipated.

Isabel was equally thankful, "I'm sure Rory would be happy that the people who done this to him are going to get their just desserts. I'm glad it's over."

"I'm pleased that I was able to help. When you came to me, Mrs. Kilpatrick, I really expected to hand the money back. I didn't think I would be able to help."

"You put yourself in such danger, I didn't mean for that to happen. I wouldn't want your mother feeling like I do."

"I put myself in the danger, I should have passed what I had on to the police."

We chatted for the rest of the visiting hour about Rory. Mrs. Kilpatrick reminisced about his childhood before his Dad's problems. Isabel spoke about how they had met and fallen in love. I could see that their shared memories were bringing them closer, as if finding the reason for Rory's death had broken a barrier that had built up as a result of losing him.

Before they left, they both thanked me again and bent over me to kiss my cheek, Mrs. Kilpatrick's tears of appreciation splashed gently on my face. She apologised but I didn't mind.

On the second afternoon Lou and Maria arrived. They both looked strained from the funeral that had taken place the previous day. Maria was still dressed in black, her face, a younger reflection of her mother's, was lined with the tension and heartbreak of the previous week. Lou looked a little better than his sister but the effects were still obvious to me.

"Craig, how are you?" Lou asked.

"I'm still a bit sore but I'm making progress."

"Li told us what happened. You shouldn't have done that. You know that mum would never have wanted anything bad to happen to you."

"I know but I felt I owed her that. I needed to do it myself, for her."

"Did he mean to kill her?" Maria seemed desperate to know, to try to understand what happened.

"I don't think so. He was in over his head and was worried about getting caught. He had his own elderly mother to look after and he was frightened that she would be left alone if he was locked in prison. Your mum disturbed him in my flat, he panicked and knocked her over as he was running away."

"I'm glad he's dead." Her bitterness was understandable but I couldn't agree. I had wanted him to face a jury and fully understand what he had done to a man who was his friend, what he had done to the Capaldis but that satisfaction had been taken from me by his death.

"How was the funeral, I'm sorry I couldn't make it?"

"OK. The priest said some nice things about Mum," Lou replied. "It was a nice service."

The conversation was staccato and full of small talk. They left after 15 minutes

Carol came into the room after they left, she had been waiting in the hall while the Capaldis were in, not wanting to interrupt our discussion. She kissed me hard on the lips and tried hard to hug me without hurting me. Then she looked at me angrily.

"What were you doing you idiot?"

"Sorry," was my pathetic response.

"How could you do this to me? How am I supposed to keep the pretence of casual indifference if you have me worried out of my skin and have me blubbing like a baby?" she choked on tears as she spoke.

"I take this means you care for me?"

"Of course I do, you stupid lump of man that you are." She leaned over and kissed me again. When she stood up again I was wearing my stupidest grin.

"Don't you grin at me, after everything that you've put me through." She playfully hit my good arm.

"Believe me, I didn't plan it this way."

She asked me for the details of what had happened and I gave her an edited version of events in the warehouse. She reacted with shock when I told her how Stone had died and how close I had come to following him. During our discussion she let slip that she had been at my bedside during the two days following the confrontation. I realised that this was going to be something a bit more than a casual fling. She left at the end of visiting time. I slept until the guys and my mum arrived for evening visiting.

Mum hugged me and told me she loved me while the guys stood to the side and let her talk.

"Oh, Craig, are you going to be OK?"

"Yes mum, the doc said that I might need some physio on my arm when it heals but I should be fine. I'll even have a nice neat scar."

"Well it looks like we'll be having Christmas at your place."

I smiled, "As long as I don't need to do the cooking. I'm sure Li or one of the guys will help you with the shopping."

"Aye, no problem Mrs. C," Paul responded.

The atmosphere was lighter than it had been the previous night and when the nurse confirmed that I would be allowed out the next day it made it even better. Li promised to come and get me in the morning, he would leave the shop to his assistant for an hour or so.

I left the hospital at ten the following morning, Christmas Eve, and Li drove me home. My mother and Carol were there to greet me, it looked like they were already forming an alliance that would be sure to cause me problems in the long run. They took turns fussing over me during the day, making sure that I was never short of coffee for very long.

I spent Christmas Day with mum in the flat, she made a delicious meal which tasted even better after everything that had happened. Carol came round on Boxing Day and I enjoyed a relaxing time, lying on the couch with her, watching classic movies.

Mum went home the day after Boxing Day, leaving me with warnings about behaving myself and doing what I was told by the doctor.

It felt good to have nothing more to worry about than which coffee to choose or what film to watch and I could feel the energy begin to come back. The rigours of the case seemed a distant memory and my relationship with Carol blossomed in the solitude we enjoyed during the holiday period.

I wondered about whether my career had taken a new direction and if I would be happy that it had. Only time would tell.

THE END

ABOUT THE AUTHOR

Sinclair Macleod was born and raised in Glasgow. He worked in the railway industry for 23 years, the majority of which were in IT.

A lifelong love of mystery novels, including the classic American detectives of Hammett, Chandler and Ross Macdonald, inspired him to write his first novel, The Reluctant Detective. The Good Girl is the second novel featuring Craig Campbell. Alaso available a third novel called The Killer Performer and a Kindle exclusive novella called The Island Murder. Sinclair has also created a spin-off series featuring Alex Menzies.

Sinclair lives in Bishopbriggs, just outside his native city with his wife, Kim and daughter, Kirsten.

The Reluctant Detective returns

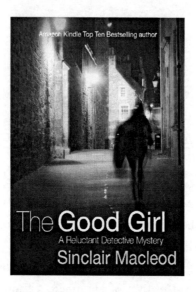

The Good Girl
A Reluctant Detective Mystery
Sinclair Macleod

Craig Campbell leaves his native city to investigate the disappearance of a young woman from St Andrews. Initially, it appears to be a simple case of a girl escaping to start a new life but it soon becomes apparent that there are ominous undertones.

When a woman's body is found on a nearby beach the case takes an even darker turn. Craig focuses his attention on the seedy world of escorts and their clients. A pimp with a violent history and a number of witnesses with their own secrets to protect block his investigation.

He finally breaks through the wall of lies and discovers a gruesome truth that leads to a dramatic and explosive climax.

Available in paperback and Kindle ebook

Death, Drugs and Rock 'n' Roll

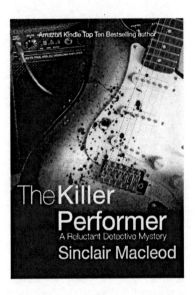

It should have been Craig Campbell's dream job, working for a rock star who was his boyhood hero. But when the target of his investigation is murdered, Craig is the prime suspect.

Despite the police suspicions, The Reluctant Detective is released and begins his own pursuit of the killer.

His investigations bring him to the attention of a Glaswegian drug lord with a vested interest in the case. Craig's own safety is threatened and he is ready to walk away but as the body count mounts he feels compelled to continue the hunt.

Rival drug gangs, jealous musicians, a disturbed rival and a crazed voice from the past are all possible suspects. Craig must find the killer before the finale of their murderous performance brings the curtain down on another life.

Available in paperback and Kindle ebook

One man will stop at nothing to find the human soul

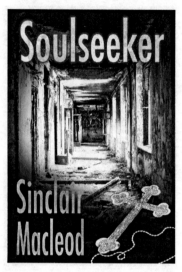

Detective Inspector Alex Menzies starts her first day in a new job with a call to the scene of a terrible murder. The body of a young man has been left on a funeral pyre with a hole in the middle of his forehead. The investigation into the bizarre murder is lead by Alex's new boss Detective Superintendent Tom Russell.

A vicious, bigoted racist is the first suspect but within days the city is shocked by the discovery of another mutilated and burned body. The killer's signature is a small cross placed in the victim's hand and the terrifying possibility of the city's first serial killer in over forty years gives the police investigators a challenge that will tax all their skills and combined experience.

The killer continues to find new victims and with each death the case becomes more puzzling and the police more desperate. As fear grips Glasgow, the investigative team must find the Soulseeker before he kills again in his search for the truth about the human soul.

Available in paperback and Kindle ebook